Even before the door to the lobby opens, I have rehearsed in my mind how I'll handle Mama when she arrives.

Under no circumstances will I show that I'm upset.

The door inches open. I hold my breath. Even without seeing her, I can picture Mama's face.

Instead, the tall figure in front of me is in ordinary go-to-the-office clothes, slightly wrinkled, a short-sleeved shirt and khakis.

"Alex?"

Of all people!

For a second I think I might sink to the floor from embarrassment. Then Alex says in an offhand way, "I guess you've been waiting awhile."

"When they took me away, I thought I'd committed a felony," I say. "I thought it was assault with a deadly weapon."

Alex shakes his head. "A hammer is a deadly weapon. A tire iron is a deadly weapon. But a gift basket? It's only a misdemeanor."

Ellyn Bache

began writing freelance newspaper articles when her four children were small. As they got older and gave her more time, she turned her hand to short stories. It took her six years to get her first one published. Then, for many years, her fiction appeared in a wide variety of women's magazines and literary journals and was published in a collection that won the Willa Cather Fiction Prize. Ellyn began her first novel, *Safe Passage*, the year her youngest son went to school full-time. That book was later made into a film starring Susan Sarandon, and Ellyn went on to write other novels for women, a novel for teens, a children's picture book and many more stories and articles. There's more on her Web site, www.ellynbache.com.

THE NEXT NOVEL™

Raspberry Sherbet Kisses

Ellyn Bache

RASPBERRY SHERBET KISSES

copyright © 2007 by Ellyn Bache

isbn-13:978-0-373-88132-1

isbn-10:   0-373-88132-0

This edition published by arrangement with Harlequin Books S.A.

® and TM are trademarks of the publisher. Trademarks indicated with
® are registered in the United States Patent and Trademark Office, the
Canadian Trade Marks Office and in other countries.

TheNextNovel.com

 HARLEQUIN®

PRINTED IN U.S.A.

From the Author

Dear Reader,

Have you ever heard of synesthesia? If not, you might think I made it up to suit LilyRose Sheffield's story—but I promise you I didn't. Synesthesia is a rare, fascinating linking of senses that lets a small percentage of people "see" sounds and "taste" shapes. Some scientists believe we could all do this once, but gradually lost the ability over the millennia. Whether that's true or not, synesthesia is so uncommon today that it's no wonder people think LilyRose is crazy when she admits that the emergency broadcasting system tone makes her see orange or that the best lemonade tastes like cool columns of glass.

It's also no wonder that LilyRose gets so sensitive about her "condition" that she keeps it a secret for more years than she'd like to admit.

In her heart of hearts LilyRose knows synesthesia is a gift… an extra dimension of experience that helps define who she is. And she knows that isolating herself to keep from getting hurt also isolates her from the people she wants to be close to…the people she might otherwise love. I hope you'll find in LilyRose's journey a story about the way all of us learn to accept and embrace our "differentness"— and discover the joyful freedom of being ourselves.

Ellyn Bache

CHAPTER 1

Yes, that's me in the photo, LilyRose Sheffield, Merchant of the Year, age thirty-five, owner of Bountiful Baskets, being led out of my shop in handcuffs, with the Gift Baskets For Every Occasion sign clearly visible on the storefront in the background. Now everyone in town will know where not to shop.

And that's Dinky Lopak—Officer Dinky Lopak—former paperboy and high school football star, currently defender of the peace, his beefy hand clutching my upper arm in a deathgrip suitable for the FBI's Most Wanted. Dinky's expression is grim.

Local Shopowner Arrested For Assault, the headline in tomorrow's *Fern Hollow Reporter* will read.

I won't see it until I get out of jail. No matter, I can already imagine it: LilyRose Sheffield, enemy of the people. She'll fix you a nice gift basket, sure, but be careful or she might turn around and bop you with it.

The photographer snaps one more shot and hurries off. As Dinky maneuvers me into the back seat of the cruiser, he leans close and whispers, "You're lucky I cuffed your hands in front instead of in back. A lot more comfortable." His cinnamon aftershave hits me like a double shot of room deodorizer. "For old times' sake," he says.

"There *were* no old times." Beyond serving as our paperboy when he was twelve and I was sixteen, Dinky and I had no relationship, unless you count the day at dawn when I caught him peering at my underwear-clad body through my bedroom window, a feat he accomplished by scaling a rose trellis and clinging to a downspout. He disappeared hastily when our eyes met, and escaped uninjured. That night I lobbed a rock into his bedroom window, shattering it with a satisfying crash. I had always had a pretty good arm. He never bothered me again.

By the time Dinky achieved the size and heft that catapulted him to high school football stardom, I was grown. Now he's a married man with three children under five, ogling me exactly the way he did at twelve. "I always knew you'd do something wacko someday," he says—a comment I find unworthy of Fern Hollow's finest. He shuts my door with a thump and slips into the front seat next to his partner.

It takes me about thirty seconds to realize that the rear seat of a police car is essentially a traveling cage, complete with doors that can't be unlocked from the inside and a barrier of what looks like reinforced chicken wire to protect the officers in the front from the perpetrator behind them. It also occurs to me that my hands are cuffed in such a way that if I wanted to scratch my back, I couldn't. My wrists chafe from the metal. Panic rises in my throat. How did it come to this?

I choke down my terror as we head down the street. At least they haven't turned on the sirens. In the interest of maintaining control, I push my mind back to the day twelve years ago when all this started—the pivotal event I thought would save me.

I close my eyes and force myself to breathe deeply.

I have to start at the beginning.

CHAPTER 2

Okay. The beginning. The day Jeremy Taylor and I broke up. An event that still makes me so mad I can almost forget my handcuffs.

I was twenty-three. Practically a baby. In *love*. I had picked up Jeremy from work because his car was in the shop, and the first thing he did was turn the radio to that loud rock station he liked, where the music was so thick it always made me see an oatmealy gray mush in front of my eyes.

"Didn't you ever hear the rule saying the driver gets to decide what to listen to?" I asked, trying to sound flirty instead of irritated.

"Oh, honey," he crooned, running a finger over the side of my face with a lightness that was more tease than touch. Goose bumps shivered all up and down my arms, and I forgot the radio entirely. I couldn't help it. Call it hormones, immaturity, stupidity; in any case, being close to Jeremy about took my breath away. I concentrated on the road and tried not to notice his strong, square jaw out of the corner of my eye. Or the blacker-than-black stubble on his cheek, which I thought was the most masculine facial feature I'd ever laid eyes on. Or the dimples that softened his expression every time he smiled or spoke. I was a fool for Jeremy's dimples.

The oatmeal-mush music throbbed on for a while. Then suddenly the Emergency Broadcast System tone came on, and as always happens when I hear that high, whining sound, everything in front of me turned such a bright orange that the road was barely visible. "Shut that off!" I yelled. "I can hardly see!"

Jeremy switched off the radio. He stared at me hard until I turned to face him. His dimples flattened into a disapproving pout. "What does the Emergency Broadcast System have to do with what you can see, LilyRose? When you say things like that, you sound half-crazy."

Half-crazy! I was about to blurt something sharp and snippy when the Sheffield vow of silence cut me off, slicing through my brain in the oft-repeated words of my mother, Zee: "Say something even once, and it's out there forever, honey. You can't unsay it. Can't control it. All it can do is hurt you."

Believe me, I knew. But under the pressure of Jeremy's less-than-loving gaze, it also occurred to me that after four months of serious dating, and especially after the discussion we'd almost-but-not-quite had about where our relationship was going, the man had a right to some information. "I've got something to show you," I told him. "Something I want to show you right now. It's at Mama's."

Jeremy groaned. Ignoring him, I made a U-turn and headed for Cardinal Circle.

The house where I grew up and where Mama still lives is a big, rambling, old-fashioned place with a swing on the front porch and a backyard that in those days was full of Daddy's flower beds. Inside, there's no central air, just window air conditioners in some of the rooms and ceiling fans in the rest. I knocked once and then yoo-hooed for Mama as I led Jeremy through the open front screen and down the hall to the kitchen, where Mama was making herself a salad for dinner. Daddy was gone until the end of the week, an independent trucker who owned his own rig and hauled the loads himself.

Mama stopped slicing tomatoes and looked up

with a quizzical expression, focusing first on me and then on Jeremy and back again. "Well," she said. "What brings you two here? Let me get you some nice, cold tea."

I held up my hand to stop her. "Mama, I've decided to show Jeremy those magazine articles." I adopted my best professional tone, which in those days was anything but convincing.

If Mama had her doubts, she didn't voice them. She raised her eyebrows, set down the slicing knife, and without a word went out to get her file of clippings about synesthesia.

Synesthesia. I hated that it sounded like a disease. It isn't a sickness. Synesthesia means having two or more senses linked—your vision linked with your hearing, say, so that every time you hear the Emergency Broadcast System tone, you see the world through an overlay of orange. Some of the articles said synesthesia affected one percent of the population, most of them women. Some said one person in every two thousand. In any case, not very many. No wonder people didn't know about it. I told myself not to blame Jeremy just yet for saying I was half-crazy. He'd change his mind once he finished reading the articles Mama set out on the dining room table. He'd apologize in his most penitent tone, all dimples and remorse.

I had been eleven or twelve before Mama found that first write-up about synesthesia in one of her women's magazines. Until then Mama and Daddy and I were as ignorant as everyone else in not even knowing it had a name. What we did know was that I saw glass columns when I tasted mint, and golden spheres whenever old Mrs. Leona Richie sang the Star Spangled Banner at a ball game or public meeting. Those things had been happening for so long that none of us thought it was unusual, but even so, it was nice to find out I wasn't the only one.

Much as we liked synesthesia's having a name, Daddy hated as much as I did that it sounded so ominous. "Sinas *what?* Sin-ess *thee* zee-ah?" He would act as if he couldn't pronounce it at all, then snap his fingers and say. "Oh, *now* I know what you're saying. *Sinus*. You're talking about LilyRose's *sinus* problems."

He became an expert at joking in this way, and sometimes it was a good thing. For example, Mama's roast beef usually made me see the kind of tan-and-white marble arches I'd seen in movies about fancy villas in far-off countries, but not if it didn't taste just right. Once, when she served an overcooked roast to company, I blurted out in front of everyone, "Why, Mama! The arches in this meat are all flattened out!" Daddy laughed before anyone could even register shock, and said with a chuckle, "Oh, there goes LilyRose's sinus problems acting up again." He sounded so casual that no one ever thought to question how a roast could have arches or what that had to do with sinuses. They just assumed that impaired drainage must affect a person's sense of taste more than they knew. This kind of incident happened all the time.

Then the day arrived when Mama's article collection became our weapon in the war against my reputation. I think all along we'd known it would come to this. Without Mama's arsenal of clippings, I might have ended up in jail long before the ripe age of thirty-five.

Not that what happened was in any way my fault. One morning during my freshman year of high school, Roy Wilson came over while I was standing at my locker and for no good reason kissed me hard on the lips. I should have pushed him away. I meant to. I didn't like Roy. Once, in the cafeteria, he had said in a loud voice to Megan Burnside, "Come over here, chubby cheeks. Let's talk about you and me getting together Friday night." Now, I could understand Roy wanting to get together with Megan. She was pretty. She was nice. She was so far out of Roy's frame of reference that he had a nerve even speaking to her. But she did have chubby cheeks. Her cheeks puffed out like a chipmunk's when its mouth was full. It didn't make her unattractive—this was hard to describe, because it didn't sound logical, but the sweet roundness of her face actually made it more appealing. You had to see her to understand. But chubby—well, yes, there was no denying it. Roy's whole table of wannabe football players started chuckling at the idea. Megan ran out of the cafeteria in tears. Even if Roy Wilson had been a person I would have chosen to kiss before then—which he was not—the incident with Megan would have changed my mind.

But there I was, getting books out of my locker for English class, only to turn around just as Roy's face was bending toward my own, everything happening so quickly I barely had time to think, oh, yuk, before his lips were touching mine. They were much softer than I would have imagined, and there was an agreeable little tug at the bottom of my belly.

But the most amazing thing was the raspberry sherbet color that appeared in front of my eyes. Well, not just a *color*—this was what I could never explain—but all the pleasant *essence* of raspberry sherbet, all its pinky-purple lightness and summery taste, as if raspberry sherbet were not just a color or even something nice to eat, but a *philosophical concept* impossible to describe in words. With all that going on, there wasn't time to push Roy Wilson away. I just stood there looking at the raspberry sherbet and liking it.

A second later Roy finished kissing me and strode off, all his buddies giving him high-fives and slapping him on the shoulder. My best friend, Dorrie, who had walked up just in time to witness the incident, was gape-mouthed with horror.

"Are you all right, LilyRose? Why are you staring into space like that?" Dorrie shook my arm. "He didn't hurt you, did he? If he hurt you, I don't care how big he is, I'm going to find him and kick his butt."

The idea of hundred-pound, five-foot-two Dorrie kicking anyone's butt snapped me out of my reverie. "He didn't hurt me," I said. "It was just…so weird." Then, in a rush of emotion, I blurted out every detail of the color-and-taste-and-lightness show that had passed before me during Roy's kiss—a tale I knew the minute I finished did not translate well into words and was something most people were simply never going to believe.

"LilyRose, anyone who sees raspberry sherbet at eight in the morning must be doing drugs," Dorrie said, with such trembling concern that I thought she might burst into tears. "Tell me you're not doing drugs," she whispered.

"Of course not. I'd never do drugs. What do you take me for?" I wasn't sure if I was more offended by her lack of trust or her lack of belief. I tried to laugh it off, but Dorrie crossed her arms and looked stern. Next thing I knew, I was being called out of class to see the guidance counselor, Mrs. Paxton. Dorrie had rushed to Mrs. Paxton's office the minute she'd left me, sobbing that she felt terrible ratting on her best friend, but she was sure I needed help. Wasn't there room for me in the school's drug abuse program? Well, of course there was. Although Dorrie later told me time and again she'd acted purely for my own good, it was a long while before I forgave her.

Mama had to bring her stack of articles to school to convince Mrs. Paxton I wasn't having drug-induced hallucinations. "It's normal for synesthetes to hear and taste things in color," she informed the guidance counselor. "It's normal for them to see shapes in front of their eyes when they experience certain sounds and flavors and emotions. This is not some…"

"Psychedelic experience?" the counselor offered.

"Not at *all*." Mama snapped herself to attention. "Compared to the general population, people with synesthesia have a whole extra set of senses. Something the rest of us could probably use." Despite her unwavering smile, Mama's tone made clear that Mrs. Paxton could probably use an extra set of senses herself, if she was so foolish as to think I needed substance-abuse counseling. I didn't breathe easy until Mrs. Paxton signed the paper to release me from the drug program, and slid it across her desk into my hand.

In the car on the way home, Mama said softly, "All you have to do is keep your mouth shut, honey. Then no one will ever know you might be feeling or seeing something that's different from what they experience, themselves. Some folks are so afraid of anything different that they'd torment it out of existence, if they could. And you know the best way to keep from giving them anything to work with?"

She raised her hand from the steering wheel and made a zipping motion across her lips.

I nodded. In my mind's eye, I could picture the nasty smirk on Roy Wilson's face if he ever found out his kiss had made me see raspberry sherbet. He had about as much ability to deal with that information as a garden slug. I raised my hand and repeated Mama's gesture, zipping my lips shut, taking my personal vow of *omerta*. I was silent about my "condition" from then on.

Silent, but not unfeeling. Catastrophic as it was, that raspberry sherbet moment (I am ashamed to admit) was so compelling that it brought on a boy-craziness as powerful as a fever in the night. I didn't want to kiss creepy Roy Wilson again, or think I'd have to. The way I saw it, my raspberry sherbet experience with him was more like a preview of coming attractions than the feature presentation itself. What I needed was someone more suitable to take his place, someone I *wanted* to kiss, whose lips would bring raspberry sherbet to my eyes and the sweet tingling in my belly that went along with it. I wanted the whole package.

It always surprised me, what attracted me to a certain boy. It wasn't usually his looks. In that respect, Jeremy Taylor was an exception. No: with Sandy Thompson it was his gravelly voice that always gave me such a shiver of delight; with James Albertson it was the loose-hipped walk; and with Jimmy Lee Sanders it was the way he was forever trying to smooth down the cowlick in his bright red hair, which always popped right back up.

I knew my boyfriends in those years weren't the ones most other girls would pick. Dorrie would say sometimes, "But LilyRose, what can you possibly *see* in him?" The truth was, I had no idea and didn't much care. There was something sweet about every one of those boys. I liked all of them. Some of them I might even have loved. But as nice as it was to go places with them and get to know them better, as nice as it was to sit in out-of-the-way places and kiss and touch and…well…as nice as all that was, not once did I experience raspberry sherbet at the touch of their lips. Sometimes I saw a sort of melty orange ice that reminded me of the sticky Popsicle ices that used to drip on my hands when I was little. Sometimes I saw a sharp lemony gel that put me in mind of Mama's lemon meringue pie, which everyone raved about but which I always thought needed more sugar. But raspberry sherbet? Never.

These were not sensations even the most level-headed person could describe without fear of ridicule. So for the whole nine years from the day in high school when Roy Wilson kissed me until the day I brought Jeremy Taylor to Mama's house, I didn't mention raspberry sherbet to another soul. True, it was a quest that consumed me. True, the continued disappointments only added fuel to my unstoppable attraction to boys and later, men. But I was steadfast. Even as I clung to my little remaining nub of hope, I remained silent as fog. Even Dorrie finally seemed to forget what had happened.

Jeremy Taylor sat in Mama's dining room for close to an hour, thumbing through her stack of articles. I helped Mama peel carrots until there were way more of them than she'd eat in a week. I went out back and brought in some marigolds and zinnias from Daddy's garden. I arranged them in a vase. I began to think Jeremy was going to stay in that dining room forever. Finally he appeared in the doorway, looking all wrung out. *Serves him right*, I thought, for the way he treated me before. I waited for his apology. He stood there for a long time.

"This…this *synesthesia*," he finally said, pronouncing the word as if it were an obscenity.

"LilyRose, I think this synesthesia might be worse than crazy."

"What?" I couldn't believe what I was hearing.

"I mean, seeing things just because you hear a certain sound…" He shook his head and let his expression go flat. "It doesn't seem like there's any treatment for it, either. It's weird."

"Weird!" I yelled, spurred suddenly into action. "Why, it's like finding out I'm the only one who sees colors and everyone else sees just black and white. It's a wonderful thing! A *gift*."

"Except when the Emergency Broadcast System comes on," Jeremy sneered. "Then you can hardly see to drive."

"It was a figure of speech! I always see through the colors just fine!" I made myself take a breath. "But if my driving is a problem for you—as obviously it is—then I guess you better start walking home. I surely wouldn't want to put you in danger."

"LilyRose…" Jeremy wheedled.

"I'm serious, Jeremy."

He cocked his head and gave me a deliberate, dimpled grin, as if to call my bluff. I pointed to the door. "Out."

That wasn't quite the end of it, but the upshot

was, Jeremy did walk home that day. Mama asked me to stay and share her salad, but I wasn't in the mood to eat. "You'd think I'd done something awful," I said. "Why don't people *know* about this?"

"They're starting to, honey," Mama assured me. "There are books on synesthesia now. There weren't any back when you were in high school. Nowadays you can read about it on the Internet, too. Why, there was even that segment on 60 *Minutes* not long ago."

"Yes, but people still think it's crazy, as Jeremy so aptly pointed out. Let's face it. I'm a freak." My eyes welled with tears.

"Oh, honey." Mama crossed the room to take me in her arms.

That sent me into an outright sobbing fit, which made me feel better but didn't change a thing. After all those years of silence, Mama was still right. The minute people knew a thing, they would twist it any way they wanted to. And even after all that silence and all those boyfriends—especially Jeremy—I'd ended up the way I supposed I'd always known I would. Alone.

One thing some synesthetes see is pain, and right then, I could see it very clearly in front of my eyes: a thin, metallic, vertical line.

CHAPTER 3

I am wrenched out of my reverie by a sobering sight. The police station. Or rather, the fact that we get there and *drive right past*. It's all I can do not to gasp so loudly Dinky will think I need to be subdued. At the very least, I thought we would stop at the police station for me to be booked. At the very least, I thought I'd get my one phone call. But no: we are heading straight to the jail.

I will be put in a cell with a roach-infested cot and a toilet in the corner. I will breathe dank air rife with lethal viruses and bacteria. I will be dead before midnight.

Tomorrow morning, instead of seeing my picture on the front page of the paper, I will be lying face-up on the cold concrete floor, my mouth open in the stiff, rigor mortis O of my last tortured breath.

LilyRose Sheffield, dead at thirty-five.

The air-conditioning in the cruiser is blasting. I begin to shiver. I'm about to hug myself for warmth when I realize I can't because of the handcuffs.

Get a grip, I tell myself.

Don't make a fool of yourself in front of Dinky.

Stop shaking.

Go back to the beginning.

So I push my mind back from the passing streets that take me ever closer to incarceration. I make myself stop wondering why I never learned more about legal proceedings than the details of the real estate closings for my store and my house. I plunge myself for warmth into the hot tears of twelve years ago, the week after Jeremy's departure. Each night I'd sobbed until my eyes swelled into unsightly red puffs. Each morning I'd applied my makeup with great precision before I dared to go to work. Heartbreak aside, my position as assistant manager of Bonnie's Baskets made it unwise to go around looking like one of Bonnie's cute creations had thrown me into a depression.

The owner, Bonnie O'Dell, had hired me the year before as a gofer. She did everything else herself. Dreamed up ideas. Decorated the delicious cakes and cookies she baked. Arranged the goodies artfully among an explosion of tissue paper and bows. My job was to pick up supplies and explain to customers how Bonnie would custom-design whatever kind of gift basket they wanted, and have it hand-delivered to hospital patients or new mothers at home, or sent by mail to college kids away at school. These were the simple tasks she thought I could do.

Then came the day she asked me to sample an angel food cake she'd made but didn't think was rich enough for a gift basket. One bite, and oh my! Although not rich like fudge or brownies, as angel food cake it was as good as it gets—a delicate pink shimmer in front of my eyes, halfway between pastel and magenta. "If I were you, I'd put samples out on the counter for folks to try," I suggested. "You'll be selling it in no time!" And of course she was. Before long it got so she'd turn to me first if she wanted to try out a new recipe or a new idea, and wouldn't even think of adding a new item to inventory without my say-so.

Not that she knew why she depended on me so. Heaven's no! And I wasn't about to tell her. Soon she promoted me to assistant manager. Before long she was using my ideas for some of the baskets, like Back to the Beach, with a bottle of sunscreen nestled between sailboat-shaped cookies. But my most inspired creation was the heart-shaped cake I suggested for Valentine's Day, with raspberry icing and candy kisses on top.

"Why *raspberry?*" Bonnie wanted to know. "Strawberry I could understand, or cherry."

I shook my head at the idea of those common flavors. "Everybody does strawberry and cherry. This would be something different. Something unique. You could call it Raspberry Sherbet Kisses." I was so persistent (without letting on why) that Bonnie gave in. She said later how surprised she was Raspberry Sherbet Kisses became so popular so fast, and sold just as well in summer as it did at Valentine's Day.

So when I came into the shop the day after Jeremy's departure, with too much cover-up on the bags under my eyes, Bonnie didn't criticize my appearance. She just looked worried. "What on earth has happened to you, LilyRose? Are you okay?" I swear, actual tears came to her eyes at the news of my misfortune—or maybe at the prospect of losing business if I became incapacitated. I was never sure.

That week was too busy for me to obsess about Jeremy until I got home at night. But when Saturday came, I had the whole day to dwell on our breakup. It was all I could do to hold myself together. I watched a dozen sappy love movies on TV, going through boxes of tissues as I sobbed my way through the happy endings Jeremy and I weren't going to have. By Saturday night I had such a headache from crying that I fell asleep at ten o'clock and didn't stir until morning.

Awful as I felt, it occurred to me to spend the day in bed. Then I thought how disappointed Daddy would be, so I got myself up.

Ever since I'd moved out of Mama's house, except for the months Jeremy and I were together, I'd gone over nearly every Sunday morning to help Daddy with his garden. It was his grand passion. All winter Daddy studied seed catalogs, and each spring he planted—phlox and hollyhocks that poked their heads above a riot of marigolds and zinnias, tomato plants that wound their way up the sturdy stalks of sunflowers, cucumber vines that snaked through beds of daylilies. Some of the Garden Club ladies snickered at this, but you'd be surprised how interesting the effect could be, more often than not.

Sunday was Daddy's only dedicated gardening

day. He always had errands to run on Saturday after his week on the road, driving his truck. On Sunday, gardening relaxed him, and gave him an excuse not to go to church with Mama.

"The only cathedral that speaks to me directly, Miss Zee, is right out that back window," he would tell her, pointing to whatever was in bloom. Mama would pretend to be exasperated, but we knew she was just as happy going to church with her friend Jamene from next door, who would tolerate far more gossip than Daddy would.

On that particular Sunday morning I didn't even try to hide my blotchy face with makeup. It wouldn't fool Daddy, and I'd just sweat it off in the sun.

I know he heard me come into the yard, but he pretended to be so busy trimming a rosebush that he didn't notice me until I spoke. "Hey, Daddy."

He lowered his pruning shears and said, "Hey, sugar. Glad you could make it. Heard you had a rough week." I knew he wouldn't come over and hug me, for fear it would only send me into tears, which it would have. Daddy hated blubbering.

"Rough week," I agreed.

"Well. Nothing like hard work and hot sunshine to make you feel better." He gestured to a bed of dahlias that needed weeding, and went back to his task. Every now and then I caught him looking over to check on me, but I pretended I didn't see.

Daddy and I had always been gardening buddies. When I was little, he'd taught me that A wasn't just for apple, but also for aster, B for baby's breath, C for cornflower. It pained him that most people didn't know the difference between a cosmos and a coreopsis, or care. After all those years of planting and mulching and weeding every week, during the months I was busy with Jeremy, I had actually longed for my Sunday mornings slogging around in the garden. That was another thing Jeremy would have sneered at, if I'd told him.

By mid-morning, sweat was running down my face, my knees were covered with dirt, and my fingernails looked as though they'd never be clean again, since I couldn't resist the feel of the soil on my fingers. Just before noon, Mama came home from church and brought out a pitcher of iced tea so sweet it made my teeth feel fuzzy but promised to keep both me and Daddy going until Mama called us in for the big Sunday dinner she liked to fix. She opened the window so we could hear a CD as we worked, some kind of reedy flute music that drifted out into the summer air and made green pyramids float in front of my eyes.

Daddy drained his glass and set it on the table. "Well, sugar, you've been through a lot this week, and you're only twenty-three, but your being here shows you're learning the most important lesson."

"Oh?" I smiled because I knew what he was going to say, and also because it tickled me how he would always fidget in some way while he was giving his lectures, pulling off a glove, shaking it as if it had something in it, putting it on again.

"The most important lesson? Why, you know it as well as you know your own name, girl. You can't wait for somebody else to bring you flowers. You got to grow your own garden."

"Yes, and pull your own weeds," I said, teasing at first and then getting an image in mind of Jeremy Taylor, weed.

"Yes, ma'am, pull your own weeds."

We spent another half hour working. Despite the shock my system had endured that week, by the time Mama called us to eat I was hot and hungry and feeling about as good as a person can feel. I dumped a last basket of weeds onto the compost heap and marveled that a person could recover so quickly—

although I knew I'd feel miserable again once I got back to my little apartment and had time to think.

"Come on, you two," Mama called again. Listening to the last strains of the flute, its green pyramids floating out into the bright garden, suddenly I thought to myself, well, why *do* I have to be miserable just because I'll be going home alone? The truth was, much as I enjoyed the music I was listening to right now, that was about how much I'd disliked Jeremy's music—that nasty oatmeal-mush rock he'd turned on in my car, which had made me feel half-sick! Come to think of it, I hadn't liked his music even in the heat of passion, when he thought he was being romantic by putting on a CD in the background, never asking what I might like to hear. As to Jeremy's kisses—not only had they not brought raspberry sherbet to my eyes (that went without saying), but they had conjured up only a dingy, mustard-colored fluff.

Maybe it was being so tired after all that work, but the whole idea of Jeremy and his music seemed repulsive. I didn't need Jeremy. I didn't need him to bring me flowers or anything else. And if my quest for raspberry sherbet was as hopeless as it seemed to be, why did I need a man at all? I would grow my own garden. I would devote myself to my career.

Until that moment, I had never thought being assistant manager at Bonnie's Baskets was exactly a *career*. But why couldn't I turn it into one? It seemed almost like fate when, the very next week, the part-time boy who took packages to the post office and the hospital stopped showing up. I told Bonnie I'd take on those tasks myself. I stayed late every night. What else did I have to do?

That was just the beginning. After that it seemed like my life followed a sort of path. I'd pretty much taken over the running of the shop when Bonnie's mama got sick, and she decided to do most of her baking at home. Then the health department tightened its rules about what kind of kitchen you had to have to bake commercial goods, and Bonnie started to lose interest, just as I was learning to stock the baskets from various bakeries and confectioneries that had come to town. The saddest part was after Daddy's accident, when he left me what he called "seed money" to help me stock my garden. I didn't think any good could ever come of a thing like that. But only a few weeks later, Bonnie told me she was thinking of closing the store. It was almost as if Daddy was winking at me as I offered my seed money to buy her out.

Like I said, it seemed like a path. I used the special talents my synesthesia had given me, but I didn't talk about them. I went out with men but didn't expect anything from them. Getting intimate was all right. Getting serious was not. The focus of my life was on my business. At the beginning I didn't know—well, of course not—that one day I'd own the shop myself, change the name to Bountiful Baskets, and become the youngest woman in Fern Hollow ever to be named Merchant of the Year. But then, I also didn't know the other thing: that one day I'd veer off the path as badly as I had today, and end up locked in a police car taking me to jail.

When we stop in front of the innocuous-looking redbrick building that is actually Fern Hollow's detention center, a big lump of dread settles in my throat. Dinky opens my door with a curt nod that means I should get out. He doesn't grip my arm so tightly this time, probably because we are within earshot of reinforcements. LilyRose Sheffield, potential escapee.

"I thought we'd go to the police station first," I mutter shakily. "I thought there were…procedures."

Dinky gives a short laugh. Very funny. He is such a cretin.

Inside the jail building, there is a long hallway leading back to what I suppose are the cells. There is also a table with a phone. "You can make one call," Dinky tells me, although of course I can't, because of the handcuffs. He dials Mama's number for me and holds the phone to my ear. She doesn't answer, which is odd. Usually she's home at this time of day, making dinner for her tenants—an activity of which I do not approve but will keep quiet about for now. I leave a message on her machine.

Dinky hangs up and guides me toward a door with a frosted-glass panel on which is printed the word *Magistrate*.

"The *procedure*," he informs me, exaggerating the word to mock me, "is to be charged by the magistrate. And the magistrate's courtroom—" he points to the door in front of us "—happens to be right here." He turns the knob and lets us in.

Inside is an informal mini-courtroom, where a man I don't know sits behind a long wooden table. There's another table where Dinky and I sit. The magistrate tells Dinky to remove my handcuffs, which is the best thing that has happened all day. Then he asks Dinky to tell him what happened.

Dinky repeats the story told by Bitsy Eversole, the victim, including her assertion that her shoulder will never be the same. Then he tells the magistrate that my assistant, Angela, said it was all an accident. Then the magistrate turns to me. When he asks if I want to give my version of the story, all I can think of are crime shows on TV, and how you shouldn't say anything until you have a lawyer.

I can't even open my mouth. Mentally, I'm back in the store again, hearing the *thwunk* of the Have Fun at Camp basket against Bitsy Eversole's shoulder. I want to blurt out that Bitsy Eversole is in no way "bitsy," but rather a large, muscular woman with a tennis serve so powerful that she's sent legions of lesser players slinking back to the clubhouse after a match—a woman whose pale blond hair and delicate features can be deceptive, but whose broad shoulders could take a summer-camp goodie basket and then some, without feeling a thing. The magistrate cocks his head. "Well?"

Still, I don't say a word. I remember how I was already thinking, "Uh-oh," as the basket clattered to the floor, sending boxes of Goldfish crackers and M&M's candy (Bitsy wanted only packaged goods for her spoiled daughter, Sally Ann) in every direction. I remember our bitter exchange of words. Most of all, I remember Bitsy's unearthly wail, echoing through the store—"My *serving* arm"—as she grabbed her cell phone and dialed 9-1-1.

"No, Your Honor, I have no statement to make," I finally say. I'm not sure if you call a magistrate "Your Honor," but I don't think it matters. I'm not going to say another word until I have the most powerful attorney in town sitting by my side.

I am charged with assault. A date is set for my trial in District Court. I am released on my own recognizance. Out in the lobby, I wait for Mama, who I know will be here any minute.

Half an hour passes. If I had my cell phone or some money, I would call again to make sure Mama got my message, but in the confusion I left my purse at the store. Besides, she always gets her messages. She is fanatic about them. She will be here any time.

On the wall is one of those round clocks with a second hand, ticking like a bomb about to detonate. I chew every nail off my left hand and start on my right—me, who only last week lectured my assistant, Angela, about the importance of keeping your nails well groomed when you are in a food-service business.

If only I had let Angela go home at lunchtime, the way I'd meant to, there wouldn't have been a witness!

A witness! Thank goodness it wasn't Joey. Oh, Lord, Joey! This is the first time I've thought of her since I was arrested. Once Bitsy tells the press I hit her because of what she said about Joey, and once Angela confirms it, Joey's name will be spread all over the front page of the paper along with mine. No! This is wrong. At twelve, Joey's too young to be the center of media attention. And to think I was only trying to defend her!

Well, I've defended people before. And I've gotten angry before. But this is the first time I've broken that cardinal business rule: never let it show.

I am such a fool.

I put my elbows on my knees and my head in my hands. I stare down at the linoleum. Little vertical lines of pain skitter across my vision.

It's one thing to destroy my own life. But Joey's?

LilyRose Sheffield, demolisher of childhood dreams.

I notice that the linoleum I'm studying is slightly soiled. I notice that it could use a coat of wax.

LilyRose Sheffield, breaker of the law. Critic of the jailhouse floor.

It occurs to me that all the mental retracing I've done this afternoon hasn't explained a thing. How did I go from the arms of Jeremy Taylor into the arms of the law in a mere twelve years? I have no idea. Why am I sitting here waiting for Mama when it's clear she isn't going to show? I can't answer that one, either. No: the only thing I've learned is that tasting things in color and making a good business of it does not keep a person from being stupid in a thousand other ways. And that is something I already knew.

CHAPTER 4

At four in the afternoon, Zee Sheffield is standing barefoot on the sticky floor of her kitchen, doing what she always does at this hour: starting dinner for her tenants. With unusual energy for a tall woman whose movements tend to be languid and steady, she snaps the stem ends off green beans she bought this morning at the farmer's market, and tosses them into her colander to wash. She doesn't think about the dizzying events of the day, which swirl around her like flies buzzing in the air. She doesn't answer the phone. She doesn't listen to the messages on her answering machine, which by now is picking up a steady stream of calls.

The one thing she can't shut out of her mind is the notion that it is probably a terrible thing for a mother to hear that her only daughter has been arrested and to feel such lighthearted relief. Shock, too. Of course she was shocked. But she was glad, because after twelve years LilyRose had actually done something illegal (for which no one in their right mind would blame her) instead of sitting there with her wings tucked in, hoping the storm would roll over her.

Zee is probably the only person in Fern Hollow— except that cow Bitsy Eversole, the victim—who thinks the arrest might be a good thing. Zee knows that she herself is responsible, at least in part, for her daughter's excess of caution these past twelve years. She knows this means her relief is essentially selfish. But she can't help it. Her daughter is about to go to jail, and she is glad.

Very deliberately, she shifts her focus back to the evening meal. Aside from the string beans, she'll make a salad with lettuce from the garden and cook pork chops on the grill, careful not to overdo the one for her elderly tenant, Leona Richie, who can't eat anything tough. And maybe she'll make some biscuits for Alex.

Better not to think about Alex right now, better to—

Before she can finish this thought, Jamene from next door bursts in through the screen as she always does, like somebody half her age, a whirlwind of motion who doesn't know how to knock. "What the *hell* are you doing here?" Jamene asks, as if Zee, not she, were the intruder. "I thought you'd be down at the station. Then I saw your car. Why are you still at home? Don't you know what's happened?"

"Of course I know what's happened. Half of Fern Hollow knows what's happened. And every one of them has picked up the phone to let me know about it." Zee viciously snaps the end off another bean.

"I tried to call you *twice*," Jamene accuses.

"I'm letting the machine pick up." Zee puts the last of the beans into the colander, sets the colander in the sink, and prepares to turn on the water.

"What's *wrong* with you? Making supper like there's not a thing on your mind! Aren't you going to bail her out? Your own daughter?" Jamene puts her hands on her skinny hips and tries to look imposing.

"I don't think so."

"What do you mean, you *don't think so?*"

"They'll let her out soon enough. A couple of hours contemplating her situation might do her good."

"How do you figure *that?*" Jamene sniffs.

Instead of answering, Zee turns on the water and begins to wash the beans.

Jamene strides over and turns off the spigot. "What about Joey?" she demands. This is Jamene's twelve-year-old granddaughter, visiting for the summer. "Did it occur to you that knowing LilyRose is in jail might upset *Joey?*"

Zee studies her friend. A small, wiry woman in her mid-sixties, Jamene doesn't have a single gray hair or wrinkle, which is irritating to Zee, who is fifty-nine and has both. "I doubt LilyRose is actually locked up in a cell, Jamene. It doesn't work like that." She sets the colander back on the counter. "Is Joey really upset?" Unlike most girls her age, the child seems totally unflappable.

"I haven't seen her yet," Jamene confesses snippily. "Roberto's mother invited her for dinner. She's still off playing that math game with him."

"Sudoku. It's not really math." Zee isn't sure about this. Maybe it *is* math. But she's anxious to put Jamene on the defensive. All she knows is that Sudoku is a puzzle where you try to fit the numbers from one to nine in a series of rows and columns and boxes, using each number just once without repeating. Zee doesn't see how an adult can do it, much

less a twelve-year-old. While other kids swim or
play ball, Joey and Roberto—who is only ten—
make a spectacle of themselves by copying puzzles
from books in the library or downloading them off
the computer, and working on them in the park, at
the library, or in some other public place. It doesn't
help that Joey is very pale and nearly bald and
Roberto is black-skinned, startlingly blue-eyed and
an acknowledged math genius.

"When Joey gets home," Jamene says with exag-
gerated patience, "she'll say she's proud of LilyRose
for being brave enough to defend her. Then she'll
go to her room where no one can see her, and cry
her poor eyes out because LilyRose is in jail. This
wouldn't be necessary if you'd go down there and
bail her out and bring her home."

"In a little while, maybe. Right now I'm starting
dinner." Zee bends to open the cabinet where she
keeps the pots and comes up so fast she nearly bangs
her head on the edge of the counter.

Jamene ignores Zee's narrowly averted concus-
sion. "Yes, Joey will probably lock her door and weep
until she either falls asleep or Alex comes in to talk
to her," she intones. Alex is Joey's father, Jamene's
son-in-law, and for the rest of the summer, because

of a complicated set of circumstances, Zee's tenant. "Alex can always reason with her," Jamene mutters.

"Oh, stop it." It's hard to picture Joey, with her hair growing back from baldness and her uncanny, un-preteen-like confidence, having a crying fit.

"Stop it? That's easy for *you* to say. Zee Sheffield, hard-hearted mother of a soon-to-be-convicted criminal, who refuses even to bail her out!"

"I told you, she'll be okay. Besides, LilyRose isn't a child. She's an adult who worries too much. Who doesn't open herself up to things. She worries *unduly*. Maybe this will loosen her up."

"So, for that reason you're leaving her down there to rot?"

"Oh, for heaven's sake, Jamene. She's not going to *rot*."

"Just go, Zee." Jamene points a skinny finger at the door. "I'll finish your damned dinner for you."

Zee turns on the water again and fills the pot. "Very generous, but I'm okay here. I'll go in a bit."

"You're a cruel woman, Zee. And a fool, too." With that, Jamene pulls down the stretchy bright orange tee that covers her flat chest, and storms out of the kitchen.

The screen slams with such an echo of angry

finality that Zee very nearly cries out, "No! Wait! Come back! I'm doing this for a reason!" Jamene is one of the few people who know about LilyRose's synesthesia, LilyRose's arrested emotional development, LilyRose's psyche in general. She's one of the few people to whom Zee can confide everything—but not, obviously, right now.

Zee turns on the stove, adds a few bouillon cubes to the water in the pot and dumps in the beans. She hates thinking about the part she played in making her daughter what she is now. Back before the raspberry sherbet incident in high school, LilyRose was like the little pig in the fairy tale who built a house out of straw, knowing it wasn't very strong but not caring much. Then came Roy Wilson's kiss and the drug program, and Zee was foolish enough to tell LilyRose to keep her mouth shut about her synesthesia. She'll never forgive herself for that. With one zipping motion of her fingers across her lips, Zee turned LilyRose from a carefree straw-house pig into a cautious twig-house resident—although *not*, thank goodness, a completely wolf-tight one, considering her interest in boys. It wasn't until that lunkhead Jeremy Taylor in sheep's clothing blew away her twig house in a single blast that LilyRose walled herself up in a sturdy house of bricks, where she'd been living ever since. And where she'd be far likelier to rot than in the Fern Hollow jail.

LilyRose is a case of arrested development. Other people don't see it because she's so successful. LilyRose's idea is that if she can't control the little squares and circles that rise before her eyes when she hears certain kinds of music—Zee thinks of this sort of like Lawrence Welk's bubble machine on early TV—and if she can't help seeing raspberry sherbet when some clodhopper kisses her, then at least she can control everything else. She can be collected. She can hide her feelings. She can have acquaintances but no close friends because she has her secret to protect, and she can tell herself she doesn't care. She can go from being a hot-blooded mama of twenty-three to a cool businesswoman of thirty-five, keeping her emotions and her men strictly on the side.

Not that Zee's not proud of her daughter. Why, at the dinner where they named LilyRose Merchant of the Year, Zee thought she'd plain float away with happiness. She felt that way until LilyRose walked up onto the stage and it occurred to her how nice it would be if Cy could have been there, watching his daughter accept her award with all the grace and glamour of a movie star.

But even for someone as successful as LilyRose, a brick wall is a mighty heavy thing to carry around in your heart.

The water in the pot begins to boil, and Zee turns down the heat. Maybe Jamene is right. Maybe she's heartless. But no. When you are as old as Zee is, you realize that the two most important things in life are being happy with who you are, even if you have synesthesia, and finding someone to love. Until today, LilyRose didn't seem likely to do either.

Maybe most of all, Zee wants LilyRose to find someone she loves as much as Zee loved Cy, whom she met when she was just eighteen, on the most humid day of the summer, at the big barbecue in Lakeside Park. They each held sandwiches in their hands, the sauce dripping down their T-shirts while they looked at each other. Then Cy uttered, without meaning to, an almost-inaudible, "Oh," as in, "Oh, *you* are what I've been waiting for all this time," which sealed it for both of them. From that day until the morning Cy drove his truck into a ditch to avoid a car full of driver-ed students that pulled in front of him, and for the sixteen days he lay in the hospital with a broken neck before he died, Zee had loved Cy with a kind of melting, all-consuming love that if she's honest about it hasn't left her even now, all these years later. She wants that for LilyRose.

As for self-acceptance, she's not asking LilyRose to shout, "Synesthesia!" off the rooftops. She just wants LilyRose to feel that, if she had to, she could.

And if none of that happens, Zee is not sure who will be the most heartsore. LilyRose herself. Or her mother.

That is her fear.

And…well, there's this. Zee also wants to tell LilyRose about Kent Oliver. She wants to be able to say she's seeing an ex-tenant without LilyRose having a fit. Unless this arrest changes LilyRose's attitude a whole lot, she doesn't dare.

But Zee has the feeling that today's events must be a breakthrough. When a person of great outward control clobbers a rude customer with a gift basket, what else can you call it? A crack in the wall. If only she doesn't seal it before the clear air of honest emotion seeps in.

This is why Zee will not bail out LilyRose. This is why she will stay here cooking dinner. No matter what.

CHAPTER 5

Even before the door to the lobby opens, I have rehearsed in my mind how I'll handle Mama when she arrives, even if she brings Jamene with her for moral support. Mama will stretch out her arms, saying as she comes toward me, "Oh, LilyRose, I was so *worried*"—as if I were ten instead of thirty-five—and she'll practically smother me in a hug. She has always been a hugger. I'll squeeze back long enough to be polite, then step away to show she's overreacting, and ask in the lightest possible tone—as if it's a joke—why it took her so long to get here.

Under no circumstances will I show that I'm upset.

The door inches open. I hold my breath. Even without seeing her, I can picture Mama's face, pinched and closed the way it gets when she's troubled. I imagine Jamene close behind her, the beat of her nervous fingers drumming against her bony thigh.

Instead, I find myself staring at a male face so unexpected that for the first second I don't recognize it. Another policeman? Coming to announce a jail sentence, after all? Then it sinks in that the tall figure in front of me is not in uniform but in ordinary go-to-the-office clothes, slightly wrinkled, a short-sleeved shirt and khakis.

"LilyRose?" He says it as though he doesn't quite recognize *me*, either.

"Alex?"

Of all people! Not only did Mama not come, herself, she sent Alex Rivers, Joey's father. A *tenant*.

For a second I think I might sink to the floor from embarrassment, scotching my mature, Merchant-of-the-Year facade entirely. Then Alex says in an offhand way, "I guess you've been waiting awhile. Okay. Let's go"—as if retrieving me from the jailhouse were no more remarkable than picking up his laundry or stopping to buy a birthday card. I follow him outside into what's turning into a drizzly afternoon, feeling myself let go of my embarrassment a little more with each step. It's an emotion Alex doesn't seem to own, so what's the point? But mainly the act of walking out into the open air, unfettered, renders me unable to feel anything but a kind of helpless joy. Who *cares* if a tenant picked me up? Even under the gray clouds, it seems like a day of great, glittering, silver magnificence.

We're pulling away in his Honda Accord before I recover my manners. "I'm sorry about this," I say, in a voice that sounds more like a croak than an apology. "My mother shouldn't have sent you down here. She should have come herself."

Alex turns to me, apparently puzzled. "Zee didn't send me. Jamene did."

"*Jamene?*"

"I was in the middle of a programming glitch when she called. I told her I'd come as soon as I could."

"You mean my mother didn't speak to you at all? Just Jamene?" I adopt my clarification-for-the-confused-client tone but realize the one who needs clarification is me.

"Just Jamene."

It occurs to me that Alex is telling the truth. A freelance computer techie who boards at Mama's but rents an office a few miles away, he certainly *looks* like someone frazzled from a rough day. I know from Mama that as soon as he gets home, he changes out of his work clothes into T-shirts and shorts. Obviously, he hasn't been there yet.

"For all you knew, you were going to have to post bond," I say. "I couldn't have you doing that. Someone should have—"

Alex raises a hand to dismiss my concern. "It's okay. Rumor has it that you got arrested while defending my daughter. This is the least I can do."

He sounds so sincere that, for the first time in the month since he arrived, I regard him as something other than *Mama's tenant,* a species more loathsome than toxic mold. He looks pretty harmless—sort of a younger, slightly better-looking Bill Gates, with that same uncoordinated way of moving that says he was never an athlete, dark hair that flops limply onto his forehead, and geeky glasses with tortoiseshell frames. I remind myself that unthreatening looks are no guarantee that he's harmless.

"So," he says, seeing that I'm studying him. "Tell me what happened."

"There's not much to tell. I had words with Bitsy Eversole. I lost my temper. It was stupid. I've been in business long enough to be able to handle a customer."

"These 'words'—were they about Joey's hair?"

"It started being about the foolhardiness of her

hanging around with Roberto. It *escalated* into the hair."

"Ah."

I close my eyes, remembering all too clearly how Bitsy described Roberto as "that strange little black boy," and how I snapped back, "Hispanic," although he's of such mixed ethnic origins that I'm not sure. "And not so much strange as a math genius," I'd told her. I'd wanted to add, "accounting genius, too," but figured Bitsy wasn't interested in a ten-year-old's ability to correct an error in my bookkeeping that I'd been working on for weeks.

"And you defended them," Alex says, bringing me back.

"If you call hitting Bitsy in the shoulder with a gift basket a defense." I give him the details. He already knows Joey often drops by the store, sometimes with Roberto but usually alone, whenever she gets tired of doing puzzles. By the time she'd watched me tie bows and arrange beds of tissue paper for half a dozen baskets, she knew how to do it herself.

"Not everyone combines a talent for Sudoku and a gift for gift wrap," I tell Alex, and watch a flush of pleasure spread across his face.

Then we get back to the crime. Bitsy has seen

Joey in the shop lots of times. Roberto, too. Why she decided to comment on my choice of companions today, I'm still not sure. "Insulting Roberto was bad enough," I say, "but what really infuriated me was her saying she couldn't understand why Joey was bald when she didn't even have cancer! Imagine!"

Alex actually flinches. "She said that?"

"Verbatim." I tell him everything, including the thud of the basket against Bitsy's bulk and the way she grabbed her meaty shoulder as if it had been ripped from its socket, then recovered fast enough to seize her phone with that same arm and dial 9-1-1.

"When they took me away, I thought I'd committed a felony," I say. "I thought it was assault with a deadly weapon."

Alex shakes his head. "A hammer is a deadly weapon. A tire iron is a deadly weapon. But a gift basket? Just simple assault. It's only a misdemeanor."

"It was bad enough, even so. I've never been arrested before."

"And is it true your assistant told the police it was an accident?"

I groan. "Did Jamene tell you that, too?" Well, of course she did. Word gets around. "Angela told the police that in the confusion I lost my grip on the basket and Bitsy got in the way. I did let go, but not until after I smacked her good. Angela knew that."

His profile registers just the hint of a smile. "That's a good quality, to engender such loyalty from your employees that they lie for you." There's a warm, russet-colored tone to his voice that signals approval.

But it's precisely then that my euphoria drops into a gray lump on the floor of my consciousness, leaving behind a raw vision of what I'm up against. "The policeman told the magistrate Angela's version of the story in as much detail as he told Bitsy's," I say. "And the magistrate charged me with assault. What does that tell you? It's obvious whom he believed."

"Not really. It's the magistrate's job to listen to the plaintiff's worst-case scenario. The idea is that justice will prevail when you get your day in court. Do you have a lawyer?"

"I will have." I pinch the skin between my eyebrows, trying to rub away the tension. "I go to court on the exact day I have a bridal-shower basket and a baby-shower arrangement due."

"Your lawyer will get the case continued," Alex says. "Delayed to a better time."

"Good." I settle back against the headrest. A

small, throbbing pulse begins to rev up behind my eyes. "I never liked Bitsy, even before," I say.

"Ah." The russet tone is comfortable, an unmistakable, *oh, yes, I've been there myself, I understand.*

"Bitsy was a year ahead of me in high school. Socially in a whole other stratosphere, and star of the girls' tennis team, which was nationally ranked. We weren't exactly buddies." I rub the bridge of my nose more energetically, but the throbbing doesn't ease. "Bitsy's not much to look at now, but she was nice-looking then, with this pale blond hair that made her look like some vestal virgin instead of the Wicked Witch of the West. And she always had a tan."

"As opposed to the Wicked Witch's characteristic greenish tint?"

"Exactly." I grin, aware that I sound like the adolescent I was twenty years ago, venting poison to a stranger, but there's something in his tone that keeps me talking. "Whenever she saw me she'd put on a smile that was supposed to make me think she was shining down on me like the sun." I wave a hand at the dreary sky. "And I was the little worm in the garden, supposed to be grateful for her warmth."

"I've been a victim of that a few times myself,"

Alex says. "The relentless smile that signals a cold heart and worldly ambitions."

"Worldly ambition, oh yes!" It's the perfect description. "When I was a junior and she was a senior, we were in a history class together, where we had to write a paper about the civil rights movement for a competition. We were both finalists. I won and she came in third."

"And that was the end of the sunshine beaming down on you," Alex guesses.

"For sure. After that it was frosty stares. She spread the word around that I'd cheated on my essay. It wasn't true, and nobody believed it, and that made her madder. Bitsy's friends wouldn't even acknowledge my presence when we passed in the hall. Then she graduated, thank goodness, and we didn't see each other for years."

"Until your unlikely reunion today?"

"No. After I bought the store, she started coming in almost every week to get some little thing—usually nothing as big as this basket—strutting around, asking questions, taking twenty minutes to buy some three-dollar trinket. I always got the impression the idea was, 'Here I am, successful society lady, and here you are, pathetic little merchant having to wait on me.'"

"Ah. The pathetic-little-merchant routine." Alex's russet voice warms to an amused shade of copper. He turns on the windshield wipers against the beginning of a drizzly rain.

"Well, I guess that's past tense," I realize. "Bitsy Eversole as a regular customer."

"No doubt," Alex agrees. After a second he asks, "What happened to the person who came in second?"

"What?"

"Didn't you say Bitsy came in third in the essay contest? What about person who came in second?"

I laugh. "Oh! She married him!"

"Good way to keep him under control," Alex says.

"That person was Rick Eversole, sole surviving male of Fern Hollow's premier family. So Bitsy continues to shine like the sun. While I, the worm in her garden, will probably end up with a jail sentence."

"No." Alex shakes his head. "Even if they convict you, you'll just get a fine. Maybe some community service. You're a respectable citizen."

Inwardly, I groan. The idea of being pointed out as the soup kitchen lady who's ladling minestrone to avoid jail time is chilling. "How do you know all this?" I ask.

"A year of law school before I decided I liked computers better."

"Strange," I say. Everything I know about Alex— which isn't much—is strange. Alex was married to Jamene's daughter, Stephanie, just long enough for Joey to be born. Alex and Stephanie have shared custody ever since, except during the summer, when Joey always stays with Jamene. Then last spring, Joey shaved her head for reasons that still aren't clear. Alex was worried enough to want to be near her during the school vacation, especially since Stephanie would be working out of the country. He couldn't stay at Jamene's because it was too awkward. So he rented a room next door at Mama's.

Not until we turn left into Cardinal Circle do I realize I didn't even have the presence of mind to ask Alex to drop me at the store, where I left my purse and my car. We pull into Mama's driveway and around the side where there's extra parking for tenants. I can't ask him to turn around now. The pulse behind my eyes quickens and pounds.

In the kitchen, Mama and Jamene are standing at the counter, pulling the stem ends out of strawberries for dinner as if they don't have another thing on their minds. Mama holds a de-stemmed strawberry in her hand and says in a normal voice, "Well, I see they sprung you."

This is not the greeting I expected.

Then, to her credit, she puts the strawberry in a bowl, wipes her hand on a towel, and comes over to give me a kiss on the cheek. No hug, just the kiss. "You okay, honey? I know it was a terrible day."

Where were you, then? I want to ask. "I'm fine," I snip, and prepare to unleash an account of my misadventures.

Jamene is too fast for me. "I heard Dinky Lopak arrested you," she says.

"Dinky?" Alex asks.

"His real name is Dennis. But he was always called Dinky," Mama explains.

"He *is* dinky," I say.

"Huh," Jamene sniffs. "Worse than dinky. All that boy was ever good for was ramming his helmeted head into some linebacker's stomach. He was brain-dead before he was twenty."

"He's not a boy anymore," Mama puts in. "He's married and has three little kids."

"Procreation doesn't take brains," Jamene retorts.

Mama is about to embellish on this—they could go on for fifteen minutes, Mama playing straight man to Jamene for a while and then vice versa. I've seen them do it. They even *look* like a comedy team, Mama tall and slow-moving, Jamene short and quick. I'm not going to hear, "Oh LilyRose, tell us everything." I'm going to hear Laurel and Hardy.

Then they both stop short when a reedy voice from the hallway pipes, "Are we having a sex discussion?"

"Uh-oh," Jamene whispers under her breath.

It's Leona Richie, Mama's first and permanent tenant. With her usual mincing steps, she's working her way past the kitchen to the front porch, where she likes to sit until Mama calls her for dinner.

"Nothing so interesting, Mrs. Richie," Mama says, shooting us all a warning look. "We were just talking about Dinky Lopak. LilyRose ran into him this afternoon."

"Policeman now, isn't he?" Mrs. Richie asks. "Remember when he was in that all-star football game? I sang the national anthem there." She gets a dreamy, faraway look on her face.

Except for Alex, we all nod and make assenting grunts to show we remember. Mama whisks a pitcher of tea out of the refrigerator and pours a glass for Mrs. Richie, which she thrusts into Alex's hand. "Help Mrs. Richie get settled on the porch, will you?" Mama asks him. "Dinner's in about an hour."

"Honored." Alex takes Mrs. Richie's arm and leads her down the hall.

Jamene fills four more glasses with ice, and Mama pours tea for the rest of us. When Alex comes back, we all stand around the counter, drinking. The tea is strong but not as sweet as Mama used to make back when Daddy was alive, and tastes like a dance of iridescent crescent moons. Nobody says anything. We just sip and watch Mama and Jamene throw strawberries into the bowl, as if we're engaged in some kind of ritual. By the time our glasses are empty, a mood of harmony has settled over us like a benediction. The tea has completely doused the pounding behind my eyes.

I clear my throat, knowing what needs be the next item of business, since we're obviously not going to address the "Mama, why didn't you come get me?" question right now. "A photographer came," I say in my smallest voice.

"Pardon?" Jamene says.

"A photographer," I tell her, louder. "From the newspaper. I think there was a reporter, too."

"You mean when you were being arrested?" Mama asks, more mildly than I think is warranted.

"When they were taking me away in handcuffs. I'm sure it'll be in tomorrow's paper. I'm saying this so you'll be forewarned."

Mama nods. Jamene goes still. Alex frowns. "A story in the paper? As in, all the details of the dispute, as reported to the reporter?" he asks.

"Probably," I say. He doesn't reply, but his jaw begins to work.

Jamene sees this, too, and her face registers growing concern. "You mean all the details, including about Joey?"

"I don't know." I feel helpless. Guilty, too. All I wanted to do was defend her. "I didn't talk to the reporter, but I think Angela did. I'm sure Bitsy did."

"So now," Alex says slowly, in a tight voice that turns the russet tones to ashy brown, "through no fault of her own, Joey will be featured as the 'little bald girl' on the front page of the paper."

"I hope not," I say. "But this is why I'm telling you. So you can be prepared. Just in case."

Alex's gaze is colder than Mama's tea. "I'm not sure exactly how you *do* prepare for something like this. Something that blindsides you and has the potential to invite ridicule." He stares icicles at me. "You should have thought of that."

I want to say that when an insult makes you so mad you clobber a customer in your own place of business, you're obviously *not* thinking. But after his earlier friendliness, I'm so surprised by his accusation that I just stand there, tongue-tied.

He turns to Mama. "Excuse me. I'm going up to change." He glowers as he leaves the room.

We all stare at his retreating back, stunned. I'm not sure I've ever seen anyone's mood darken so quickly. Dr. Jekyll to Mr. Hyde in a couple of seconds. If I were a parent, maybe I'd react the same way. But his behavior puts me on guard. Mama says this is crazy, but I'm always afraid for her when she has male tenants in the house. A woman alone is vulnerable, even with old Leona Richie around. Danger can come from where you least expect it.

Relax, I tell myself. The man is Joey's father. Joey is *okay*.

But Alex? We're barely acquainted. For all I know, his being here has nothing to do with Joey's shaving her head. For all I know, he's well versed in the court system not because of law school but because he's experienced it firsthand. For all I know, he's here this summer as a fugitive from justice.

Even in my own frazzled mind, this seems unlikely.

Deep thoughts by LilyRose Sheffield, criminal.

"Do you want to stay for dinner?" Mama asks. "Jamene's staying, too. Joey's eating at Roberto's."

Jamene, getting plates from the cabinet so she can set the table, visibly stiffens. Can't Mama feel the daggers of hostility aimed in my direction? Apparently not. "I invited Kent Oliver, too."

"Kent Oliver?" Great. Another tenant—well, ex-tenant. He stayed at Mama's for a month while he was on temporary assignment, before they brought him in as a permanent employee of the local plant.

"There's plenty of food. Pork chops on the grill. Lettuce from the garden." Now I know why she's not even going to ask the details of my day. She's too busy planning a dinner party.

Maybe she reads my mind. "Sit down, honey," she says. "Tell me what happened." Like always, her voice is a beige cushion, soft and comforting, but the invitation is about half a day too late.

"I'm tired," I say, although "tired" does not really describe it. "I just want to go home."

Mama doesn't argue. "Of course you do. You'll feel better tomorrow." She doesn't look me in the eye.

I won't ask for a ride back to the store. I'll walk. I'll get the spare key out of its hiding place, let myself into the closed shop, retrieve my purse, and drive back to the empty, newly decorated townhouse I bought a year ago, with a mortgage that before long I probably won't be able to pay.

"Bye, honey." Again the beige voice but no eye contact. As she speaks, Mama turns to the refrigerator and takes out a pint of whipping cream. "You did the right thing," she says to the carton.

Then why didn't you come get me? I think.

She pours the cream into a bowl, doesn't look up. Jamene has moved into the dining room to set the table. I feel like someone with spinach in her teeth, or streaks of chocolate on her dress from the spilled contents of a gift basket.

"You know," I say as I open the screen door to let myself out, "none of this would have happened if you hadn't started taking in tenants."

Mama looks up, startled. "Tenants?"

"Alex. A stranger." Tenants have always been a sore spot between me and Mama. "Coming to get me at the jailhouse. Instead of *you* coming."

Mama stops cold. "LilyRose—" she begins, but I wave her off.

"Never mind. I'm too wiped out. We'll talk about it later." And I let the screen drop closed behind me as I walk out.

There's no satisfaction in leaving like this. What's the point? Alex is angry, Jamene is angry, and by tomorrow Joey is likely to be angry, too—or worse, humiliated. And Mama is hurt. But if she really thinks I did the right thing, why didn't she come get me the minute she heard? Or at least offer some explanation for why she didn't?

I walk through the damp evening, eyes throbbing, shoes pinching, feeling—what? Responsible. Vilified. But mostly confused, because at the time, lashing out at Bitsy felt somehow appropriate. And freeing. And in some deep-down way, it still does.

I'm not even sure why. All I'm sure of is that I'm alone in this. Not solitary, which I'm used to and usually enjoy. But lonely in a way I haven't been since before I turned my life around twelve years ago— loneliness opening like a dark cave, all around my heart.

CHAPTER 6

It's only eight-thirty in the evening, not even dark in spite of the clouds, but Zee feels as if she's been awake since the dawn of time. The only thing that keeps her from dozing off right now, in the middle of unloading the dishwasher, is the feel of Kent Oliver's hands kneading the tension out of her shoulders. His mouth comes just to the level of her neck as he stands behind her. His breath on her skin is warm.

"By tomorrow everything will start to fall back into place," he says. "It's been a long day. Everybody needs to sleep on it."

"I know." Zee closes the dishwasher and turns to face him. He's been the only bright spot in the dismal evening. After LilyRose walked out, Alex Rivers came downstairs to say he wouldn't be eating, after all. He hadn't changed into his usual shorts but into a fresher version of the outfit he'd worn to work, and he was obviously anxious to be on his way. Jamene left before dinner, too— "Just to make sure I'll be home when Joey gets there," she'd said. This was the lamest excuse Jamene could have invented. They both knew that if Joey got home and didn't find Jamene next door, she'd come over here like she always did.

Zee was mighty weary of Jamene's moods. Earlier this afternoon when she'd stormed out because Zee wouldn't go get LilyRose, she'd waltzed right back in not ten minutes later, declaring that she'd sent Alex to get LilyRose "because I can't stand the idea of you leaving her there another minute." Zee meant to protest Jamene's taking matters into her own hands, but she had been so relieved that LilyRose would soon be free that she hadn't said a word. A little exposure to the jailhouse would last LilyRose a long time, Zee reasoned. What did it matter if she got out now or a few hours later? Seeing that Zee wasn't going to put up a fuss, Jamene started helping with the dinner preparations as a sort of apology. Then everything got complicated after LilyRose mentioned the reporter, and after Alex and LilyRose left, Jamene went right back into her hateful huff. It was enough to wear a person down.

After that, if not for the soggy weather, Zee would have suggested that she and Kent and Leona Richie eat on the patio. But it was too damp. They'd sat at the nearly empty dining room table, picking at what turned out to be far too much food. Even Leona, who liked being around people in general and Kent in particular, had sensed the heaviness of the mood and excused herself early.

"I thought I was doing the right thing, not going to get LilyRose," Zee tells Kent now. "I don't know what I could have been thinking."

Kent touches her hand, then kisses her lightly on the lips, something he has started doing every time he leaves. "Get some sleep, Zee," he says.

She watches from the window as he walks around the side of the house to his car. In her fifty-nine years, Zee has known all kinds of couples: interfaith and interracial and everything in between, but sometimes she thinks she and Kent are closer to *intergalactic*, they're so different in so many ways. He's a corporate engineer with two different college degrees. She has no degrees and never wanted any. She's always been a homebody. After one bumpy flight when she was forty, Zee vowed never again to get on an airplane. Kent has traveled all over the world, mostly for work.

And the way they look! Kent is short and chubby, with thin, sandy hair you can practically see through. Zee is six feet tall with thick gray hair that won't lie flat no matter what she does to it, adding at least two inches to her height. Once when he was boarding here, Kent came outside just as Zee arrived home from church in a dress and high heels, which made her practically tower over him. They are an odd couple, for sure. Not to mention that Zee is nearly sixty and Kent is fifty-three. If he hadn't turned out to be such a good conversationalist at dinner, Zee never would have looked at him except to notice that he preferred ranch dressing to French and mashed potatoes to rice. Every time she thinks she's going to tell LilyRose about him—how considerate he is, how interesting, how easily he makes her laugh—it occurs to her that all LilyRose will see is that Zee and Kent are members of two different species. She won't see them as beanstalk and gnome the way most people would, because appearances don't matter much to LilyRose. No, she'll see them as something much worse: landlady and tenant. No matter how nice Kent is, LilyRose will never see this as a good thing.

Zee watches Kent back up his car. She waves in

case he looks up, then turns out the light in the kitchen. Tired as she is, she isn't ready for bed yet, but she doesn't want to work anymore, either. The darkness will keep her from filling a couple of salt shakers or flipping through her cookbooks for ideas for tomorrow's dinner. Feeling her way through the familiar room, she settles into a kitchen chair with a view out the window to the rain-dulled dusk, and wonders why nothing has changed in the years since she first told LilyRose she was going to rent out one of her rooms.

"Oh, Mama, no! You're turning my childhood home into a boarding house!" LilyRose had laughed at first, so merrily that she obviously thought Zee was joking.

"I'm serious, LilyRose. Poor old Mrs. Richie has been talking about going into a nursing home ever since her singing voice gave out and she stopped being invited to do the Star Spangled Banner everywhere. Now, you know as well as I do that she doesn't need a nursing home. Her mind is as good as ever. She's just lonely, and her legs hurt too much to stand at her stove and cook meals anymore. So I'm renting her a room and providing her with supper."

Watching LilyRose put her hand to her throat as if she were choking, Zee had not added that her decision had been prompted by something other than altruism. Zee had been wallowing in loneliness ever since she'd finally absorbed the fact, and the finality, of Cy's death. But even worse than the loneliness was her terrible sense of uselessness. Cy, aware of the dangers of driving a truck full-time, had carried enough life insurance to leave Zee comfortable. She didn't need to work. But she hated feeling like a guest in the world with no real responsibilities. A healthy woman in her fifties needed something to do. Some purpose.

Leona Richie's plight inspired her. Zee had never expected her life to be played out on the great stages of the world, or even the greater stages of Fern Hollow. After all, she was not going to start a charity or run for office. But Mrs. Richie was someone she could help. The truth was, it would help both of them. She could stay right here, on Cardinal Circle, in the spacious, gracious rooms of the house Cy had left her, and do what she was best at: cooking and serving food, and making people feel at home.

"Where will she sleep?" LilyRose had demanded

that first day. "You know she's too frail to walk up the stairs to the bedrooms. And what if she falls? She could sue you for millions."

Zee had been cowed by her daughter's reaction, but irritated, too. "I'm going to put her in the sewing room on the first floor. It's right next to the bathroom. She'll be fine there. She'll like it. And she's not likely to fall. But if she does, I have liability insurance, just like you do for the store. I'm not a fool, LilyRose."

"Oh, Mama, I never thought you were a fool! But I do think this is foolish."

"You know, people all over the country are quitting their jobs and buying up old houses like this one, so they can turn them into trendy little bed-and-breakfasts," Zee said. "I've read three or four articles about it."

"So?" LilyRose had sulked.

"So maybe your problem is a matter of semantics. 'Boarding house' sounds tacky. Bed-and-breakfast sounds…I don't know…*entrepreneurial*. So just think of this as a bed-and-breakfast."

"Except that you won't be *serving* breakfast," LilyRose muttered.

Zee had remained firm. "Think of me as someone

starting her own business. Someone just like you were when you bought your shop."

LilyRose seemed bewildered, as if it were impossible to imagine Zee this way. "You know, Mama, I don't understand you at all." They had dropped the subject entirely for the rest of LilyRose's visit, which lasted only another five minutes.

Twenty minutes later, LilyRose called Zee from home. "You're just having Mrs. Richie?" she asked, sounding appropriately contrite. "Nobody else?"

Zee hadn't actually thought this through, but she sensed she needed to choose her words carefully. "Well, who knows? Mrs. Richie, for now. Then we'll see how it goes."

"But no men." LilyRose spoke with such authority that the hairs stood up on Zee's arms. You could not let a child dictate your life, even if that child was grown. "I didn't say, 'no men.' The plant brings in people temporarily all the time. They're always looking for places to stay."

That's when LilyRose began to seem genuinely alarmed. "Oh, Mama! You could be renting to some con man, for all you know. You could be renting to some serial killer!"

"I have a pretty good sixth sense about danger."

Actually, this was something Zee had never considered and didn't plan to. "I don't see many serial killers in my future."

"That's just the point! Serial killers look like everyone else. Seeming innocuous is their *hallmark*."

It was then that Zee knew this was not about tenants or boarding houses, but about wolves in sheep's clothing, who seemed sympathetic audiences for whatever you might want to tell them, but would use it against you if you did. The Jeremy Taylors of the world. So Zee had promised not to take in men, at least for the time being—which had been a mistake, because when the plant did call with the first potential male boarder, and Zee had said yes, she and LilyRose had had the same conversation all over again.

That was at least half a dozen tenants ago, not all of them male. Each time one came and went without incident, Zee had the fleeting hope that LilyRose would get over it, but she didn't. Zee had even halfway hoped that Alex's picking up LilyRose at the jailhouse might be the gesture of kindness that would finally win her over. She couldn't have been more wrong.

Well, no use going over all that again. Taking a

deep breath to clear her head, Zee was filled instead with the heavy scent of roses so sweet that she had to blink hard to control the flood of tears that sprang to her eyes. Cy had planted those roses at least ten years ago. Maybe more. They grew in rich profusion up the back wall of the house, blooming in perfumed abandon every June. The first year after he died, Zee was sure she'd felt his presence when she breathed in their heady aroma. But each year after that, although the scent persisted, the sense of Cy's nearness grew dimmer, finally fading entirely. The odd thing was, this had seemed exactly right. She had missed him, but somehow not needed him as much. She had felt, each year, just a little stronger. Except at times like these. If Cy were here, he'd know what to do. When it came to LilyRose, he always had. He'd had a special bond with her from the moment he'd first named her Lily, saying it was a pretty flower and easy to grow, and then added Rose after she screamed all night, claiming that roses were equally beautiful but a lot more work.

As indeed she was.

The sound of a car engine broke into her thoughts, followed by a sweep of lights through the yard, then silence and darkness again. A car door opened and closed, then the front door. Steps ascended the stairs. Alex. From the lightness of his tread, he seemed less agitated than he'd been before. Well, she hoped so.

Usually Zee didn't feel one way or another toward her younger tenants, who tended to be out most of the time, doing whatever young people do. But she'd liked Alex from the first day he'd come to look at the sunporch, the only room available at the time. They'd stood in the doorway while she told him the rent and explained that she provided supper each day, always something that could be kept warm in case he came in late.

"Does that mean casseroles?" Alex had looked so crestfallen that Zee wanted to laugh.

"Lord, no. My late husband, Cy, wouldn't abide any kind of casserole," she assured him. "Cy liked to be able to look at his plate and distinguish each kind of food sitting there. No casseroles, unless you count chili."

Alex had been so visibly relieved, so clumsily straightforward—the same way he was today when he got so upset about the newspaper possibly mentioning Joey—that Zee had felt sorry for him.

Did Alex Rivers sound like a serial killer? Like

someone who kept his sinister, inner thoughts buried deep?

Only to LilyRose. Only to a person so intent on staying safe that she saw danger in everything— except, apparently, flinging a gift basket across her store on a whim that might have been her best impulse in twelve years.

Even so, if Zee had known how this was going to turn out, she *would* have gone to get LilyRose. It had never occurred to her Alex would hurt LilyRose the way he did, acting like the reporter showing up was LilyRose's *fault*. But Zee can't exactly bring herself to blame Alex, either. Most of all, she can hardly stand to think how alone LilyRose must feel right now, as if no one is on her side. LilyRose needs a friend to turn to. But her only confidante is Zee. This seems so sad.

Yet for all that, Zee isn't about to call LilyRose and say she's sorry. In some way, in spite of everything, she's not.

Not that LilyRose would answer the phone, in any case.

This is when Zee can't stand it anymore. This is when she puts her head down on her arms on the kitchen table and begins to sob.

This is when someone touches her on the shoulder and in less than a millisecond she forms two perfect thoughts. Serial killer! LilyRose is right!

She freezes, waiting for the dagger to slice across her throat.

Her heart very nearly drums its way out of her chest.

"Relax," Kent's voice says. "It's just me."

Suddenly aware that she must have stopped breathing, Zee inhales a noisy gulp of air. "I thought you went home," she gasps.

"I started to. I came back. I had a feeling you'd be sitting here like this."

Kent puts his hand under her elbow, helps her up. "Come on," he says. "Let's go to bed."

"To bed?" This has never happened before. Zee is fifty-nine. Kent is fifty-three. Six years. Fine for close friends, but not more.

On the other hand, she knows he will hold her as long as she needs him to. Which might be all night.

Very likely, this is *all* he will do.

Or maybe not.

He puts his arm around her waist and guides her toward the stairs.

His car must be right outside her house. Anyone who comes by will see it.

This is probably not a good idea.

She doesn't care.

CHAPTER 7

You would think a person as distressed and depressed as I am wouldn't sleep a wink, but the minute I flop onto my couch, still in the rumpled and slightly damp clothes I've been wearing all day, I'm out cold. Next thing I know, the morning paper is hitting my front door with a thud. I wake up with a twinge in my back, followed by such a jolt of alarm that in spite of the pain I catapult myself upright and spring to open the door, inwardly steeling myself to face my likeness on the front page of the paper.

It isn't there. The prominent visual is an architect's rendition of the controversial new high school, set above a two-column article.

My story isn't on the front of the local section, either. It's buried three pages back, a tiny article next to the police blotter.

Oh, there's a picture, too, but it's so small it

doesn't really draw the eye. The Bountiful Baskets sign on the store window has been cropped out. Part of my profile and most of my shoulder are visible as I stoop to get into the police car, aided by Dinky's uniform-clad, weight lifter's arm.

Arrest Made In Fracas, the headline reads. That's the worst of it. That, and seeing my name in print.

Seeing that Joey's name isn't mentioned at all…that's good.

The article itself is blissfully vague. Conflicting reports have been given about a dispute between a local shopkeeper and her client. The two women apparently argued about a personal matter unrelated to the gift basket the client was buying. Ultimately, the basket was either dropped or thrown in such a way that it hit the complainant's shoulder.

That's it. Two paragraphs, and what is surely the most unimpressive photo of the dozen the photographer took.

It's true that Bountiful Baskets and LilyRose Sheffield and Bitsy Eversole are mentioned by name. But Joey isn't. No reference at all to children or baldness.

I hope Alex Rivers is enjoying his breakfast of crow. Now that the crisis he feared has been averted,

I can afford the luxury of being annoyed. What hypocrisy, all his casual friendliness as he retrieved me from the jailhouse, all his false sympathy while I rambled on about Bitsy! I'd actually been *appreciative* when he acted as if Bitsy deserved to be clobbered, which she did. Why bother being so nice if he was going to flip-flop the second he heard about the reporter? Did he really believe I wanted Joey to suffer some horrible embarrassment?

Yet my relief at the article is so profound, so much beyond what I would have expected for my own sake or even for Joey's, that I can't stay angry. Father's concern for child trumps rudeness to shopkeeper. Or some such thing. Maybe I have no choice but to be forgiving, after he got me out of jail. No matter. It's over. Time to move on.

I put down the paper, strip off my filthy clothes, and spend a blissful twenty minutes in the shower. Washing away yesterday's humiliation, I prepare as best I can for today's—people with snickering smiles in their voices, wanting to know what *really* happened, the inevitable canceled orders, the hooded glances.

When I get to the store an hour before we open, I find everything even more pristine than usual. Angela has cleaned with extra care, knowing our curious customers will hope to find the remains of the offending basket still scattered across the floor.

Carrying my cell phone with me as I make my inspection, I check my watch far too often and finally decide I've given Larry Tibbets enough time to get to his office. A few years ago, not long after he decided to make real estate law his specialty, Larry and I were "an item," as Mama used to say—although that was too strong a term. Larry is one of at least a dozen men I've gone out with these past twelve years, a dear friend even now, and more than that for a while, but never the center of my life. During the time we were together, Larry was sweet, attentive, and pleasant to talk to. His kisses were a deep maroon that reminded me of plush leather furniture, comfortable but unexciting. He's married now to a woman I don't know but feel a little sorry for. When his secretary puts me through to him, he says yes, he's seen the article, and yes, he knows just the criminal lawyer to defend me. One more phone call, and Carolyn McManus has tentatively agreed to represent me in court.

Angela arrives just as I hang up. She uses her key to come in the back door, and seems so startled to see me that she puts her hand over her mouth as if to stifle a cry.

"Don't look so scared," I say. "I only throw baskets at customers, never the staff."

She manages a sheepish smile. "It's just that I thought you might want to sleep late this morning. I mean, after all you've been through."

"Oh, Angela. You didn't really think I was sleeping!"

A little miffed, she takes the opportunity to look away as she puts her purse under the counter. "Okay. Here's the truth. I thought you might want to spend the morning in hiding. I would have covered for you."

She would have, too. Angela is a constant surprise. At first glance, she seems like a timid, round puff of a woman, who on closer inspection turns out to be affable and quite slender, with a wide, pleasant face that reassures people for reasons they can never understand. Angela has no talent at all for decorating baskets, and she didn't get her GED until last year at age forty-six, when her daughter finished high school. But she's smart in ways that have nothing to do with book learning. She'll make suggestions if customers ask for them, but her manner seems to say, "Why, anything you choose is going to be just fine!" She makes people trust themselves. I've never seen anyone walk out on her without buying something. Yet at the first sign of anything she perceives as a danger to me, she becomes the drawbridge the enemy has to cross in order to storm the castle. Did LilyRose Sheffield throw that basket? Certainly not. The whole incident was an accident.

Any employer would find this endearing.

It's troubling, too, because as good as Angela is at suggestion, she's an unreliable liar. Sometimes you believe her absolutely. Sometimes she sounds so ridiculous that you roll your eyes. "Don't you think it was risky, that story you told the police?" I ask.

"No. It's just my word against Bitsy's. I'll get to tell it again in court. I'll get plenty of practice."

"Yes, but I have a strong suspicion you have no talent for perjury. Not that you *should*. You ought to—" I'm about to lecture her about the virtues of truthfulness, but the real truth is, I'm grateful, and Angela knows it.

"Look at it this way," she says as she plucks an ad off the fax machine. "I have a fifty-fifty chance they'll believe me."

"I wouldn't count on it. Bitsy is an Eversole. The bastion of Fern Hollow society."

"Fern Hollow doesn't *have* 'society,'" Angela says, in a surprisingly insightful (but incorrect) observation. She throws the ad in the trash. "Besides, Bitsy is a bitch."

I have to bite back a grin.

We work in silence after that. Angela tends to the paperwork. I start on a Congratulations! basket, arranging neon-green and magenta tissue in a wicker basket until I realize my eyes can't take this level of brightness today and switch to pastels. Both of us jump the first time the phone rings. *Cancellation*, we read in each other's eyes. I let Angela answer. It's exactly as we thought, except that this is one of Bitsy's good friends who doesn't want her order after all. We knew this was coming. Five minutes later, we get the other friend-of-Bitsy cancellation we expected. Now comes the real waiting, to see how many would-be customers are following my story, and how much they plan to disapprove with their wallets. A couple of weeks in a real downturn, and I'm in trouble. I've already put down deposits for supplies and a refrigerated rental truck for the big barbecue and band concert at Lakeside Park later this summer. It's been a Fern Hollow tradition for more than half a century, the event where

Mama met Daddy all those years ago. Everybody comes. This is the third year in a row the town council has hired me to sell trinkets and desserts. For Bountiful Baskets, it's a major moneymaker at a slow time of year. Halfway through my now-pastel basket, it occurs to me not to count on it this time. The chairman of the council is Bitsy's father-in-law, Fred. I could still be fired.

Thankfully, just in time to save me from feeling even more morbid and depressed, the front door flies open with such force that the bell announcing customers goes into a little spasm of jingling rather than stopping after its usual single ding.

"I heard!" Joey exclaims as she strides in on pink flip-flops, her T-shirt blaring the words, Bald Is Beautiful across her perfectly flat chest. She stands before me with her hand on her nonexistent hips, possibly the only twelve-year-old on the planet who still looks more like a child of eight than a fully developed woman of twenty-five. Her blue eyes flash. "Daddy told me! Bitsy said something about me, right? About—" Joey touches her hand to her stubble. "And you swatted her!" She swats the air as if going after a fly.

"Well…not exactly."

Unfazed, she raises a hand to high-five mine. "Way to go!" Because she's obviously so thrilled, I high-five her back even as it occurs to me that the wiser course of action would be a lesson in nonviolence, anger management, turning the other cheek.

"So. Tell me everything." Joey plops herself on the bench beside my wooden work table, located in the center of the store so people can watch. I'm not sure what to say. How much did Alex tell Joey last night? Certainly he held back Bitsy's mean-spirited suggestion that Joey had no right to be bald unless she was recovering from chemo. How much does Alex want her to know?

"Well—" I pretend to be weighing the virtues of chocolate-covered raisins versus pink-and-white dinner mints for what seems now like a far-too-pastel basket suited only for infants or brides.

"The chocolate raisins," Joey says decisively. "They clash with the tissue-paper but they taste good. You can put something more color-coordinated on top of them. Mints are wimpy." She removes the bag of raisins from my hand and sets them into the basket. "I can hardly believe this! You went to jail for me! That's so heroic!"

"Heroic? Wait a minute!" I set the basket aside.

"Listen, Joey, this is serious. I didn't do anything heroic. Quite the opposite. I lost my temper and did something stupid, and I'll probably have to pay a big fine for it. I didn't go to jail, either. I went to the *building* the jail is in because that's where the magistrate sets a court date for you."

"A court date." Joey glows. "Can I go? I mean, it's a public building, right? I can go, and Roberto can go. It doesn't matter how old we are, right?"

"I don't think so." This is not going well. From behind the counter, Angela gives me a wink.

A few curiosity-seekers come into the shop just then. Three middle-aged women, but apparently no one who recognizes me because they mill about for a while, pleasantly gossiping in low voices about the "incident" that happened here yesterday. I force myself back to work, shooting Joey a warning glance before I lower my head.

To her credit, she doesn't react to anything the women say, or even to their obvious shock as they notice her nearly bald head and quickly look away. She only drums her fingers impatiently on the table—a habit she learned from Jamene—her face suffused with such high color that I'm sure she's imagining me being led away from my trial in a bright

orange prisoner's suit...possibly to life imprison-
ment, solitary confinement, execution by firing
squad.

Aware as I am that Joey is experiencing only the
cheap thrill any adolescent would feel at being responsible for an adult's near-incarceration, her excitement is so flattering that it's hard for me to keep
focused on the sobering lecture I plan to give as
soon as the women leave. Most days, when Joey
first walks into the store, I have to adjust to her all
over again. Last summer, she looked like everyone
else, a scrawny girl with thick, shoulder-length hair
Mama used to call mousy brown, with dull gray
undertones that would call for highlights and glosses
when she got older. She had always re-invented
herself each year, wearing exclusively pink shorts
one season and an Atlanta Braves baseball cap the
next. Last summer it had been four purple strands
of what she called Mardi Gras beads, that bounced
around noisily during her high-speed comings and
goings, announcing her like a necklace of laughter.

But now! Every other girl her age has developed
breasts and curves and a long mane of hair, while
Joey remains flat and skinny and, unthinkably, bald.
Well, not really bald anymore. Her hair has begun

to grow back since she shaved it before school let out. Maybe this is worse. The stubble pokes out all over her head, not long enough to soften her high forehead or disguise her slightly protruding ears. She claims she shaved her head because her mother wanted to take her to England this summer and she wanted to come to Jamene's like always, and she knew her mother wouldn't try to take her overseas if she was bald—a story nobody believes. She wears tiny gold stud earrings as if to prove she's a girl, and claims she'd wear longer, dangly ones but Alex won't let her—one thing in his favor. With her nearly naked head, it's easy to see that when Joey grows up she'll be a woman of ordinary prettiness, her thick-lashed blue eyes her best feature. In the meantime, her manner might say she's unbreakable, but her appearance is usually as fragile as porcelain.

Today is the exception. With her high spirits and high color, she's a picture of strength, even in the cheerful beat of her drumming fingers as the women circle the shop and comment at length on each basket in the display and every one of the goodies in the bakery case. In the end, they actually buy something, a dozen of the beautifully iced petits fours the previous owner, Bonnie O'Dell, still makes for the shop. The sale doesn't amount to much, but I'm glad for it. Turning any kind of profit after my disgrace is something I didn't expect.

The minute the women leave, the phone rings again. I can tell from Angela's face that this isn't another cancellation, just an inquiry of some kind. For the first second I think, *Mama*. It's about time she called to explain about not coming to the jailhouse yesterday, since we certainly didn't get it settled last night. But Angela holds the phone tightly and twirls a pencil in her fingers the way she often does when she thinks it's going to be a lengthy conversation. "Vendor," she mouths when she looks up.

I nod. Practically everyone in town who's known for light-as-a-feather biscuits or a special recipe for hummingbird cake has tried to sell us some for our baskets. We do buy quite a lot. I haven't lost my knack for tasting when a product is just right. The syrupy, dark river of Len Barnhardt's toffee. The snappy red circles of Agnes Kettle's homemade jelly beans. But right now the thought of putting out more money is scary. It's not even mid-morning, and already I realize that I'm not going to know right away how much the Bitsy incident will cost me. Small as the article was in the paper, it will take a while for word to get around, for gossip to build and people to act. Watching Angela twirl her pencil ever more urgently as she struggles to tactfully get off the phone, I can't help thinking that her reward for all her good work might well be to lose her job if the shop goes under.

Which we won't know for weeks.

Whatever I meant to say to Joey has escaped me. I must look as worried as I feel because Joey stops tapping her fingers and gently moves her hand over to pat mine. "Listen, LilyRose," she says softly. "I don't have to come around the shop so often if it's a problem for you. I mean, if it's going to make people say things that make you so angry you really *do* end up in jail."

I sense that she'd like nothing better than to come see me in prison every visiting day. She'd spend hours choosing Sudoku puzzle books to help me pass the time, or baking files into lopsided cakes, only to be turned back at the security check. The prospect of all this begins to get away from me. I force myself to stay on subject. "You know what?" I tell her. "You're always welcome in this store. Any time you get bored with Sudoku, or even if you're not. You're welcome to hang around here 24/7 if you want to. You can even help me with the baskets."

It doesn't occur to me then that Joey will take me up on this. That's how out-of-touch I am with the adolescent mind. I don't realize until it's too late that, from this moment forth, Joey will consider herself an essential member of my staff.

CHAPTER 8

"Okay. Tell me what happened," Jamene says.

"Nothing," Zee tells her. "I'm sorry to disappoint you."

"If you want, you can leave out the worst of the porn." Setting the plate with her blueberry muffin onto Zee's kitchen table, Jamene plops herself into a chair, nearly spilling her coffee.

"There are no details. Really." Well, maybe there are, but Zee isn't ready to discuss them. Can't Jamene see that?

Well, no. "I mean it, Zee. We've been friends too long for this. Tell me the truth."

"I *am* telling you the truth. Why would I lie to you?"

"Ze-e-e." Jamene drags out the word as if it's all she can do to hold onto it. "Kent's car was here at three in the morning when I got up to go to the bathroom. So don't tell me *nothing*." She tastes her coffee, makes a face, reaches for the sugar bowl.

"Kent started to go home after dinner and then came back because he knew I was upset," Zee says. "I was upset because all of you walked out on me yesterday even before we ate supper. It was rude, in case you're wondering."

Jamene isn't. "Kent came back and then what?"

What the hell, Zee figures. "He took me upstairs and held me until I fell asleep."

"He held you? In your bed?"

"Yes."

"Undressed?" Jamene dumps two heaping teaspoons of sugar into her coffee and stirs it.

"Fully clothed." Zee is tired of this. "I *told* you there were no details."

"Fully clothed but lying down?" Jamene is relentless. She adds more sugar to her coffee, sips it, nods approval.

"That's disgusting," Zee says. "A person your age doesn't need so many simple carbs. Use that." She points to a glass bowl filled with packets of Splenda.

"You know I don't like artificial sweeteners."

"Fine. Gorge on sugar. Don't complain to me when you get diabetes."

"Doesn't run in my family. Mama ate candy every

day of her life and died at ninety-one. Don't change the subject. Were you lying down, or what?"

"Sitting up against the pillows at first. Then lying down." Zee doesn't know why she's revealing all this. She wasn't ready to. Didn't intend to. "We both fell asleep."

Jamene adopts an expression of haughty disdain. "Sure. You fell asleep in your clothes."

"We *did*. I already told you that." Zee stirs her own coffee, which has been sitting on the table since before Jamene's arrival, cold and untouched. "You have such a filthy mind. I knew you wouldn't believe me."

"I don't have a dirty mind. You slept all night like that?"

"He didn't stay all night. I got up around five and he was gone. End of story." She doesn't mention the sweet note he left, saying, *Hope the new day ushers in better times. Talk to you soon. Love, Kent.*

"Well, I don't believe you," Jamene says.

"I knew you wouldn't."

This is just like Jamene, Zee thinks. She doesn't believe her about Kent, although they've been friends for so long that she ought to pretend to even if she doesn't. All she wants is to pressure Zee into revealing some juicy, X-rated details.

"Go home, Jamene," Zee tells her, picking up Jamene's plate with the freshly baked blueberry muffin still untouched.

"You don't really want me to go home. Give the muffin back."

For some unfathomable reason, Zee does.

"Sit down, Zee," Jamene says.

Zee does.

"So what does this mean?" Jamene asks. "If he held you half the night but nothing happened? What do you think it means?"

This is exactly what Zee has been trying to figure out. What *does* it mean? "I don't know."

"It means he cares about you more than you thought."

"Maybe." Zee thinks about the signature on the note: *Love, Kent.*

Jamene begins to dismantle her muffin. She breaks off one piece and then another, and lays them out on her plate as if to make sure none of them contains an unwanted foreign object. "It means he wants to sleep with you but respects you too much to try it when you're having a bad day."

Now Zee remembers why she puts up with Jamene—because she has formulated the thought

Zee has been trying to capture all morning but hasn't been able to until now, the moment the words came out of Jamene's mouth. "I'm not so sure he wants to sleep with me," she says.

"Why not?"

"I'm older than he is."

"You are?"

Zee is grateful for this, though she's already figured out that their age difference isn't obvious to most people just by looking. "Six years older. I'm an older woman."

Jamene selects a piece of muffin and puts it into her mouth. "Testosterone knows no age limits."

This is ridiculous—Zee has seen plenty of May-December liaisons, and May is always female—but it's exactly what she wants to hear. Her age isn't going to prevent Kent from wanting her. *Love, Kent* must mean that, in some way, he already does.

She relaxes for the first time all morning. She allows herself to remember the drowsy sense of worth, and sense of ease, that had come over her as she lay with Kent's arm around her and her head against his chest, listening for the first time in years to the soothing, life-affirming beat of another human heart.

* * *

Ten minutes later, Jamene rises from her seat as if jolted by electricity. "I nearly forgot! I promised I'd go in to work this morning." Ever since Zee has known her, more than twenty years, Jamene has had a part-time job doing clerical work at the senior center. Given how self-centered and annoying Jamene can be, Zee is mystified that anybody, other than Zee herself, has been able to put up with her this long. Jamene has just finished wolfing down every scrap of the blueberry muffin she pulled apart. Then, even though Jamene knows Zee baked the muffins from scratch, she said bluntly, "Not bad, but not your best, either. A little dry."

As Jamene is about to walk out the door, she still hasn't asked if Zee has talked to LilyRose since last night (she hasn't), or how upset LilyRose might be about the article in the paper (which Zee doesn't know). In fact, Jamene didn't comment on the newspaper story at all until Zee finally blurted out, "Well, did you see it?" Then Jamene only nodded and said, "Yes. Thank goodness they didn't mention Joey." Not, thank goodness LilyRose's picture was so small you can hardly recognize her. Not, thank goodness the damned thing was buried back in the paper. Not, I'm sorry for the fuss everyone made last night about reporters; we must have put LilyRose in even more of a blue funk than she already was. Not a word about any of that. Just, tell me all the dirt about Kent and let me out of here.

"See you later," Jamene says, and plucks another muffin (a too-dry, not-your-best-effort muffin!) from the serving plate to take with her. Oh, this is classic Jamene. Doesn't Zee know it! Take, take, take, and give back a crumb any time the mood strikes. Zee ought to be glad to see Jamene go, but she isn't. Now Zee has to decide for herself if she should call Kent to discuss last night or wait until he calls her like his note says he will. Not that she plans to tell Jamene about the note. But even in a roundabout way, it would be nice to have someone to confer with.

She begins to clear the dishes from the table, clumsy with irritation over her friend's rudeness. Aside from the Kent issue, she'd like to consult Jamene about how long to wait before calling LilyRose at work. Jamene is a whiz at this. She can say within a five-minute span exactly when LilyRose will be at her wits' end, worrying if Zee will ever get in touch with her to apologize about the jailhouse fiasco. "Call right then and she'll accept any kind of lame apology you care to offer," Jamene would say. "You'll have her back in a heartbeat."

But no. Jamene is off to work, a place Zee doesn't believe for a second she needs to be right now, no matter what she claims. For years she's arranged a flexible summer schedule so she can be with Joey. As long as she gets the filing and the letters done, she can arrange her hours any way she wants. The only reason she's pretending she needs to go to work right now is that Zee has given her so much gossip to mull over that she needs time to let her mind digest it. Zee has been taken in again, just as she's been taken in about a million times over the past twenty years. She shouldn't have given Jamene any damned details at all.

She slams the few dishes into the sink, including the Flower Power cup Cy got years ago at the Philadelphia Flower Show. It's a big cup that holds the heat, the only one Jamene will drink from even though she knows it's Zee's favorite, too.

As the cup hits the side of the sink, a sizable chip flies off from the rim. Terrific. It's so jagged it will probably take an hour to glue back, even with Supergrip. Zee blames this on Jamene. If Jamene hadn't had her hysterectomy twenty years ago, Zee's life would have never gotten so entangled with hers and this would never have happened. If Jamene hadn't had that surgery, the cup Cy brought home for Zee would still be intact, and Zee would be a thousand times better off.

Mentally, Zee has been through this scenario at least a thousand times. Why does she put up with Jamene? Why did she ever? Twenty years ago, Jamene had been nothing but a *charity case*. Hadn't Zee had enough to do without *that*? Jamene's daughter, Stephanie, had come to Fern Hollow to help out after Jamene's surgery, but she had to go back to college before her mother was really well. Zee would have been a heartless robot not to respond when the girl knocked on her door and said, "Mrs. Sheffield, I hate to bother you, but Mama isn't quite herself yet. I wonder if you'd look in on her now and then." The whole thing had been pathetic. Zee hardly knew Stephanie. The girl was older than LilyRose, so the two had never been friends. Zee knew Jamene only well enough to say hello as they were going in and out of their houses. You had to feel sorry for a family that had to ask for help from a next-door neighbor who was practically a stranger.

Dutifully, Zee took soup or casseroles over to Jamene every day. It turned out that the reason Jamene wasn't quite herself was because she had an infection. Zee took her to the doctor and then to the hospital for IV antibiotics and then back home. Jamene let Zee wait on her hand and foot.

Then Zee got a stomach flu so nasty she could hardly lift up her head. LilyRose, who was in high school then, got it just as bad. Cy couldn't help because he was on a long haul all the way across the country. Zee called Jamene to tell her she couldn't cook. True to form, Jamene didn't believe her. "It's because you think you've done enough for me, isn't it?" she'd pouted. "You think I've eaten enough of your chicken and dumplings to last a lifetime."

Zee could hardly believe what she was hearing, but she was too sick to be snippy. "Oh, Jamene, no. I'd make you a whole dinner right now if I felt better." The word dinner made her think she'd upchuck any second. "I'm sick as a dog and throwing up about every five minutes. LilyRose has it, too."

"I've been feeling bad all day myself," Jamene said in a shaky voice that would have gotten her the role of the dying heroine in any amateur production in the country. "I think it might be the infection starting up again. There's a pain where the incision was. I wish you'd come over just for a second and take a look at it." She added weakly, "I'd do it for you."

Zee had reached for the trash can and pulled it toward the bed, in case she couldn't make it to the bathroom. "I wish I could," she'd muttered. "But I'm afraid I might vomit all over your new Oriental carpet."

At that, Jamene grew silent. Zee knew she was really fond of that carpet.

"Well," Jamene whispered finally, as if agreeing to take on the weight of the world, "if you can't come to me, I'll come to you."

Two minutes later, despite Zee's warning that the virus was contagious, Jamene walked into Zee's kitchen without knocking, as she'd been doing ever since. In one hand she carried a can of Campbell's chicken noodle soup and in the other a box of saltines. Testing the limit of her culinary skills, Jamene warmed the soup on Zee's stove, poured it into bowls and put the crackers on a plate. Both Zee and LilyRose protested that they couldn't eat a thing, but somehow both of them did. It was the first thing either of them kept down.

Even then the relationship might have played itself out when everybody got better, but that was about the time of LilyRose's raspberry sherbet phase. With Cy gone so much, Zee sometimes felt she'd pop wide open if she didn't have somebody to talk to. One night over wine she told Jamene everything, and for once in her life, Jamene seemed to forget about herself long enough to listen. It was a secret, Zee had told her. The best Zee could figure, Jamene hadn't told a single other soul, all these years.

It's funny, how sharing a secret could bind you to a person. Sometimes Zee thinks the secret that binds a man and a woman is usually sex, and the secret that binds a woman to another woman is gossip they both swear never to tell. They'd tolerate all kinds of nonsense from each other as long as they kept that secret between them and didn't share it with anyone else. That's why extramarital affairs break up so many marriages, and women's friendships break up when one of them tells something she's promised not to. In that respect, at least, Jamene had been faithful.

Instead of tossing the Flower Power cup into the trash as she really ought to do if she had any sense,

Zee washes and dries it gently and puts it back in the cabinet, along with the chip. She will glue it back together as soon as she gets a chance. This is something she is good at.

She's not going to call Kent, she decides. She's not going to chase him.

The idea of chasing a man—the fact that this idea actually occurs to her—is ridiculous.

She picks up the phone all the same. She dials Jamene's home number. It's impossible to tell whether she's there just by looking out the window because Jamene always keeps her car in the garage. The phone rings until the answering machine picks up. Zee doesn't leave a message, but it galls her to know Jamene's caller ID will tell her Zee couldn't keep her distance.

Since the jig is up, anyway, she dials the senior center. The operator puts her through. So. Jamene wasn't lying. She's actually at work. When she picks up, Zee says, "I need your advice."

"Of course you do," Jamene says.

"Stop gloating. I just want to know when to call LilyRose. I'm sure she's in the shop right now."

There's a pause on the other end. Then Jamene says with assurance, "You can call her anytime you like. It's what you talk about that's important. Let me just lay it out for you."

Actually, Zee already knows what Jamene is going to say: stick to small talk. This is so silly. While Jamene outlines the plan she always outlines, Zee reflects on what's really on her mind. "Well, thanks," she says. "And one other thing."

"What?"

"You remember what I said about being fully dressed?"

"You were lying."

"Well, sort of."

"I knew it!"

"Don't get too excited. Nothing happened. He just wanted me to be comfortable."

"I'll bet he did."

"It was very innocent," Zee insists, though it didn't feel that way at the time.

"How innocent are we talking about?" Jamene asks.

Zee takes a long breath. "Well," she says finally, "he might have taken off my blouse."

CHAPTER 9

I wake up one morning and, all of a sudden, it's hot. This happens every year in Fern Hollow, and every year it surprises us, the dragon's breath of July sending temperatures into the nineties and rendering the air so sultry it's hard to breathe. There's no breeze. No relief even at night. People who complained it was never going to get warm blot sweat from their necks and grumble about smothering. For two weeks, everything seems to pause, stunned into motionless silence by the stifling air.

Even my life, which from the moment I pitched that basket at Bitsy Eversole's shoulder had felt like a film unraveling too fast, now feels as if someone has hit the pause button. Business doesn't pick up, but it doesn't slow down, either. My court date looms, but Carolyn the lawyer says she'll have it changed and not to worry. Is she kidding? For weeks,

Bitsy has been wearing a sling on her shoulder and telling everybody how I've ruined her serving arm forever—a claim somewhat mitigated by stories that she's been playing tennis early in the morning when there's hardly anyone at the club. Even the rumor that Bitsy has been pressuring her father-in-law to have the town council take action against me turns to nothing, though this is exactly the sort of thing Bitsy would do. I hold my breath and wait to see what she'll be up to next.

Worst of all, Mama and I are caught in a limbo where we can't stay mad at each other but can't seem to make up, either. She calls me at the store the day after my arrest—exactly as I know she will—but instead of saying what's really on her mind, she makes a point of confining herself to chitchat. "How are you, honey?" "Okay. You?" "Fine. Fine. Right as rain." *Right as rain?* She asks if the newspaper article upset me, and I say no, which we both know isn't true. She agrees she's glad the story wasn't on the front page but sorry that it was published at all. No discussion of my lonely hours at the jailhouse, or Mama's failure to end them. This is a strategy Mama employs because Jamene tells her to. I am not supposed to know this. Jamene tells her not to confront a subject directly because the longer she waits, the more it will wear me down. Most of the time, it's Mama who wears down first. Why do we do this? Aren't we adults? It's so awkward that Mama doesn't invite me to dinner for over a week. This is for the best, because it keeps me from having to make up some excuse. But I miss her even while we're making small talk on the phone.

The dense heat coats everything, holding us in place like figures cast in wax. The only thing that moves is Joey. Her constant, darting presence in and out of the shop ever since I told her she's always welcome is probably what keeps us sane. She's going to keep regular hours, she informs us, except for Tuesday afternoon when she and Roberto have to be at the public library. "We're doing an online Sudoku competition," she says earnestly. "We have to do it on the public computer. You can live with that, can't you?"

"Well, yes. I suppose so."

"Otherwise I'll be here part of every day."

I'm not one of those women who ooh and aah over kids—thank goodness, since I'm never likely to have any. But I've always been fond of Joey, at least since the summer she was three and announced she was going to grow up to be a cheetah. Mama and Jamene rolled their eyes, but Joey was serious. The adventures she devised for herself and her favorite toy cheetah so enthralled her that she was determined to join the species. When she wasn't pretending to be bounding through the jungle, she sat licking the back of her hand to clean herself. She licked so much that she wore a sore spot into the base of her knuckle. That's when Jamene stopped rolling her eyes. She worried herself half to death but never said a word to Joey.

"What if I make it worse?" Jamene lamented to Mama. "What if I damage her psyche?"

I was the one who finally had to take action.

"You can't grow up to be a cheetah," I said boldly, uttering the hard truth her grandmother had been afraid to express.

"Why not?" Joey asked.

"Because only baby cheetahs grow up to be cheetahs. You're a little girl. Little girls grow up to be women."

Joey was not convinced.

"It's true," I insisted. "Babies grow up to be like their parents. Kittens grow up to be cats. Puppies grow up to be dogs. When you grow up, you'll be a woman like Mommy and Grandma."

"Are *you* a woman?"

"Sure. What did you think I was? A robot?" I made a mechanical walking motion that sent Joey into peals of laughter. She was the only one who truly appreciated my humor. "I am the very *essence* of a woman," I said.

"Then I can grow up to be like you."

"Absolutely." Not only was I was flattered, I had saved the day. Never again did Joey claim to be a cheetah-in-the-making.

Now, by the time she starts what she seems to think is a serious apprenticeship in the store, I already know she's a quick study at tying fancy bows. But I don't realize the extent of her talents—managerial as well as decorative—until the day Angela is doing her well-meaning best to create a summer gift basket using a flower pot as the container. Angela's effort at brightness translates into wads of red and orange tissue paper stuffed into an earth-toned terra-cotta pot, the clash of colors so garish that I want to close my eyes.

Angela says, "Oh, this is a mess," and turns to me for instruction. My inclination is to give her something else to do. But Joey brings over a sheet of pale yellow paper and says gently, "You're closer than you think. Look." Lifting the red tissue out of the arrangement, she replaces it with the yellow, then finds a cantaloupe-colored sheet to replace Angela's Halloween-orange selection. When she's finished, everything complements the clay pot. "How's that?"

Angela studies the effect. "Good," she says thoughtfully. "Better than good. Great."

"Yes," Joey agrees immodestly. "Summer baskets should feel like sunshine."

Feel like sunshine? The description sounds like something I myself would say. Useful as my synesthesia has been, I've endured its perilous ups and downs far too long to wish it on someone else. Until Joey's hair grows out, the last thing she needs is another personal oddity to attract attention.

"A basket of sunshine. That's what we can call it," Angela says. "You design them and I'll name them." She seems to think they're a team.

Joey grins in my direction. I tell myself to relax. She doesn't have synesthesia; she just has a good eye. On the off-chance that I'm not in violation of some child labor law, and if the town council doesn't fire me from the band concert, I'll be grateful for her help.

"You're the only math whiz I've ever met who has a flair for design, too," Angela says. "I always thought math and art came from different sides of the brain."

Joey smiles but shakes her head. "Sudoku's not math, it's logic. This is logic, too."

I don't know about Sudoku, but I've always thought designing baskets took more intuition than logic. So I'm doubly glad to hear Joey doesn't agree. If she believes it's logic, then her mindset is probably more "bright color reminds people of sunshine" than "gee, this naval orange doesn't taste as much like sunshine as it ought to."

The heat continues to build—or at least to hold, because I'm not sure it can build any more without setting the town on fire. At the workbench in the center of my air-conditioned shop, Joey and I settle into a routine while Angela stays behind the counter to handle customers and vendors. I do the design work. Joey fills the baskets and helps me with the bows. Soon the three of us talk easily together as we work, even though Joey is so young.

We discuss the closing of the town pool due to bacteria, the price of Internet services, the trashy silver-glitter handbags all the local teenaged girls

carry this summer—"Only because the Bag Bou-
tique went out of business and sold them cheap,"
Angela informs us. "Even Mel has one."

"Mel?" Joey asks.

"My daughter."

"Why do you call her Mel?"

"Short for Melissa," Angela says. "Why do they
call you Joey? Your real name's Joanna, isn't it?"

Joey makes a face. "Yes. Isn't it awful? I told my
mom if she didn't call me Joey, I'd go on a hunger
strike."

"Joey!" I interrupt, stifling my impulse to laugh.
"You were never called Joanna a day in your life.
Your grandma didn't like the name. Jamene dubbed
you Joey before you got out of the hospital."

"Oh?" Angela looks from me to Joey and back
again.

Joey puts on an "okay, you've caught me" expression and raises her hands in a gesture of surrender.
I give Angela a wink. Joey's lies—and there aren't
many of them—always sound more like the cheetah
stories she made up to dramatize her life when she
was little, rather than an effort to fool anyone.

Two days pass before a customer regards Joey's
growing-back hair with more than its due amount

of attention. It starts with a squinting, suspicious ex-
amination of Joey's scalp, where the fuzz of a few
weeks ago has been thickening and filling in, but
not enough to look normal. Then there's the
"should I ask or shouldn't I?" glance in my direction—to which I hope my sharp return gaze signals
a firm "shouldn't." With her stick-thin build, Joey
might be a victim of illness, if her color weren't so
high and healthy-looking, and she *might* be an adolescent boy, if her earrings weren't so feminine and
her clothes so girly, in colorful pastels that always
seem to contain at least a splash of pink.

Don't, my gaze says to the curiosity-seeker, and
to her credit, she doesn't. There are a few others
after that, but they don't get out of hand, either—
although every once in a while they seem so close
that when I catch Angela's gaze she seems to be
thinking, *Oh, no, is LilyRose going to clobber someone
else?* It's a look that makes me take a deep breath
and, in one instance, walk into the back room for a
long drink of water.

On Tuesday when Joey's at the library—only the
second Tuesday since our new arrangement began—
the shop feels so empty, even when it's not, that
neither Angela nor I know quite what to do. How

do you get so attached to a bald, prevaricating preteen so quickly?

Part of the reason is that we've already begun to depend on her help. Among other things, almost every afternoon she takes all our packages to the post office a few blocks away. That afternoon, I miss Joey even more when I realize I have an out-of-town package to mail before the post office closes, even though I'm already late delivering an It's A Boy! basket to a woman home with her newborn son. The basket is an expensive one, filled with the usual toys and trinkets, but also with a few of Bonnie O'Dell's amazing ginger cookies, hand-decorated with icing drawings of diaper pins and booties and—the pièce de résistance—a baby bottle fashioned entirely of frosting. I've watched Bonnie make these, and it's a lengthy, delicate procedure. The last thing I need is for the icing to melt en route because I have to stop at the post office on the way. Right now, I just can't afford to give a refund.

In the sweltering heat, I don't dare leave the baby gift in the car while I go inside to mail the package, so I take the basket with me. As always right before closing time, there's a line. I clutch the box with one arm and slip the basket over the other, trying not to notice how the wicker handle cuts into my flesh. We're having the kind of heat wave that strangles even the most efficient air-conditioning system, so even the cavelike post office feels abnormally hot and close. But at least nothing is melting. To distract myself from my sore arm, I calculate how many gift baskets like this one I'd have to sell each month to keep the store afloat if I lose the band concert job. Too many. Ever since my arrest, the undoing of my professional life has been nagging at my mind like a buzzing fly.

Then a voice brings me back, drifting toward me in familiar, russet waves. "Well, if it isn't Little Red Riding Hood," it says.

For a second I'm at a loss, still absorbed in profit margins. I raise my eyes toward a pale, bespectacled face. Alex Rivers. He's smiling down—sarcastically, I'm sure—at the basket slung over my arm.

"And if it isn't the Big Bad Wolf," I blurt out.

Brilliant. I sound as if I'd like nothing better than to engage in suggestive repartee. For an encore I might as well start batting my eyelashes. It's entirely to Alex's credit that his laugh comes out sounding like silver sparkles and not nasty little red darts.

Before I can stop him, Alex reaches over and takes

the postal package from my hand, allowing me to move the baby basket and restore circulation to my arm.

"I'm glad I ran into you," he says.

"You are?" The man who practically accused me of sabotaging his daughter's life is *glad he ran into me?*

"I am."

Amazingly, the line speeds up just then, and we reach the front. Alex walks me to the window, sets the package on the counter, and gallantly relieves me of the baby basket as I pay my postage. As glad as he claims to be to see me, that's how not-so-glad I am to see him. I've been dreading his response when he hears that Joey is spending hours each day at Bountiful Baskets. I'm pretty sure he doesn't know and wouldn't approve. How Joey has kept the secret for almost two weeks, I'm not sure. The one benefit of not making up with Mama or having to go over there for dinner is that I can't let the news slip out over a dish of homemade peach cobbler, and then have to watch Alex rise from his place, slam his hand on the table and stomp out.

"I'll walk you to your car," he says when I'm finished. Still holding the baby basket, he follows me outside into tropical heat that slams into us like a physical force. I've never been to Africa, but I'm sure this is what it feels like.

"I meant to get in touch with you before this," he says when we're both able to breathe again. "I over-reacted that night at your mother's. I would have apologized sooner but I've been out of town." He must catch my not-quite-believing-this look, because he adds quickly, "Sometimes they send me out of town to troubleshoot software."

"Oh."

Alex's expression looks hopeful. I'm not sure what he wants. A word about accepting his apology? Or a little groveling? Why, Alex, you saved me from the jailers! No need to apologize!

I don't do either.

"Did you get things set up with your lawyer?" he asks as we walk down the block. "What did he suggest?"

"She."

"She," he corrects.

"I like her." I know how belligerent I sound, as if I'm defending her from a sexist comment he hasn't actually made, but I can't help it. "She makes me feel (a) intelligent despite the fact that I don't know the legal lingo, and (b) worthy of representation."

"Does she think she can get you off?"

"She isn't sure."

Alex nods. "Yours is an interesting case, in some ways. I looked up some precedents."

We reach the car. Although he hands over the baby basket, he makes no move to leave. He stands awkwardly for a moment, then leans back against the car door, only to reconsider when he touches the hot metal.

"Precedents?" I prod.

"Oh. Yes." He proceeds to tell me more about my case than Carolyn did, including previous decisions that included everything from perjury (it's scary to picture Angela as a perjurer) to fraud.

"And all this interest comes from your abortive years of law school?"

"More from my great prowess as an Internet researcher," he says, with the same silly air of bravado I've come to expect from Joey.

Now that I see Joey every day, I notice how much she resembles him. They have the same narrow face, the same pale skin, the same thick lashes above large, round eyes, although Joey's are blue and Alex's hazel behind his glasses. It's hard to tell yet whether Joey has inherited her father's lanky frame, but easy to see that she's better coordinated than he is. For the first time, I notice that Alex's right shoulder rides slightly higher than the left. This must be why he always looks a little off-kilter. Whether there's some physical reason for this or whether it's just the way he carries himself, I'm not sure. It's one of those small flaws I often find endearing in people, and I halfway wish I hadn't noticed.

Alex doesn't seem aware that I'm staring at him, which is a relief. He's so engrossed in the court case, so immersed in his research but also so egoless about it, that I think, *Why, he's done this because he's still protecting Joey*. He doesn't want her name to come up in court. It seems like the nicest thing.

I don't expect what happens next. I never would have predicted it. A swift, unbidden twinge of desire tightens at the bottom of my belly, a little rush of pleasure.

I want to censor it, but it's too late.

Where did *that* come from? Desire is not an issue here. Alex is being helpful, nothing more. Until this moment, the most lascivious thought I've had about him is that, under other circumstances—if he were not Mama's tenant, if he had not put me in his debt by rescuing me from jail, if he had not pretended sympathy and then turned on me—we might be friends.

The twinge is gone as quickly as it came, but I won't forget it. I never do.

"Did she get the trial continued?" Alex asks.

It takes me a second to focus enough to answer. "She wants to. She says a delay will give her more time to prepare. But I'm not so sure it's a good idea. Sometimes I think I should just get it over with."

"What do you mean?"

"Let Bitsy have her day in court and move on. I'll have to plead guilty anyway."

"Plead guilty?"

"Well, sure."

Alex's voice darkens. "No. You can't."

I *can't? Can't* seems pretty strong, maybe even dictatorial, but I let it go. "Carolyn told me the worst that can happen is that I'll be fined. That's exactly what you told me yourself. She even says community service isn't likely. She says—"

"That's not the point."

"If that's not the point, what is?"

"Pleading guilty would be giving Bitsy something she doesn't deserve."

"Well, of course it will give her something she doesn't deserve. What Bitsy deserves is to be buried slowly in sand."

I hope he'll smile, but he doesn't.

"Why do you care?" I ask.

"Nobody wants to see a person rewarded for insulting their kid." By now his voice has lost every bit of its warmth, descending from russet to ash-brown to dirty-ice-gray, as if the temperature has just dropped seventy degrees.

Just as I did at Mama's, I feel foolish for having been taken in by his amiable facade, but this time it doesn't leave me speechless. "Nobody wants their child to be insulted. I don't want to be insulted, myself. But if the outcome is going to be the same no matter how I plead—"

"No." He raises an open palm like a stop sign. "Don't plead guilty. Don't give in." And then, still in that icy-cold tone, "I have to go."

Sometimes your manners take over even when you don't mean them to. Instead of getting in the last unfriendly word, I hear myself saying, "Well, thanks for the help."

Maybe this confuses him. Maybe he's only trying to confuse *me*, because just as he turns away, he adds, "Take care," in the warmest shade of bronze.

As I open the door to my car and slide the baby basket onto the seat, I realize I've been standing in ninety-degree heat for at least ten minutes, mesmerized by a man who, despite his confusing vocal cues, probably dislikes and distrusts me. I am such a fool! He's had me so rattled that I've never even checked the heavy basket I lugged all the way into the post office to keep cool.

Heart in throat, I look down to see if the baby-bottle icing is melting.

It is.

But only a little.

Inside the car, I turn the air-conditioning as high as it will go, and aim the vents at the basket. I decide that the line of frosting marking the edge of the baby bottle is only slightly runny, not enough for a sleep-deprived young mother to notice. Certainly not melted enough for a refund. I drive away into the sly, hot air, determined to concentrate on business.

But all the way to the young mother's house, all I can think about is that unexpected, unwanted, telltale skitter of pleasure low in my belly, not five minutes before.

You work so hard to get your life under control, LilyRose...and then this.

This is how your body betrays you.

CHAPTER 10

On Sunday morning at 7:00 a.m., the shrilling of my bedside phone jolts me out of a heavy sleep. I want to answer, but my head hurts too much to open my eyes. My tongue feels too swollen to talk. My mouth tastes exactly like the Fern Hollow Grill, where I spent way too much time last night with Colby O'Brien, who has been a friend for years but never a boyfriend. Colby has just lost his job. I'm afraid of losing my business. We commiserated.

Normally, I don't drink much. To me, any kind of hard liquor tastes like spikes, though I never mention this. Beer is a sudsy washbasin, and wine runs the gamut from mud puddle to raging river. Last night's pinot noir was a lazy current, easy going down. I'm so thick-headed this morning that the first thing I do is stretch an exploratory arm onto the other side of the bed, just to make sure Colby isn't there. He isn't. Maybe I drank too much, but I didn't entirely lose my mind. I pick up the phone.

"Hello?" I murmur in my husky hangover voice.

"LilyRose? You all right, honey? You sound sick."

"Not sick, just sleepy, Mama. It's early. What's up?"

"LilyRose, I hate to ask, but it's so hot I know nothing will get done if you don't come over right now. That's why I didn't wait until later to call you."

"Call me about what, Mama?" I manage to sit up, having seen that I had the good sense to put a full glass of water on my nightstand. I down it in a single gulp.

"Your daddy's flowers," Mama says. "They're about to worry me to death. The leaves on the roses are turning black and those annuals, the ones that look like bright-colored daisies, but taller—you know I can't ever remember the names of flowers…"

"Zinnias?"

"Zinnias! Yes. They look awful. You'd think somebody painted their leaves with whitewash. I really need you to come take a look."

"It's this heat," I tell her. "The zinnias have mildew."

"They do?"

"They get it most every year. I guess I forgot to spray."

"Can you get rid of it?" she asks.

"I can try."

Despite the hangover, I'm out of my house in fifteen minutes. This is not because the roses and zinnias can't wait. It's because I know this isn't really about flowers.

Mama hates air-conditioning. She doesn't turn it on until she's about to melt, and anyone who walks into her kitchen knows why. Although the room is cool, the old window unit grinds away like a waterfall, so noisy you need earplugs after the first five minutes. Mama is standing at the counter flipping through the newspaper, not in her usual old jeans but in new capri pants and a yellow shirt she usually saves for shopping. I know I'm the one she got dressed up for. "I wanted to see you face-to-face," she says, which I also know. She comes over to hug me. I let her, not meaning to hug back. But I do hug back. Then both of us pull away, braced for the showdown.

I mean to let Mama speak first, but before I have time to think, I blurt in the most untactful way,

"Why didn't you come get me out of jail? Why did you let that—" I point up toward the sunporch where Alex sleeps. "How could you let some *stranger* come get me?"

"I didn't know he was getting you until he was on his way," Mama says. "Besides, you weren't in jail. Just the jail *building*."

"The jail, the jail building, same difference." I can't believe I just hugged her. "How could you just *leave* me there?"

"I don't know, LilyRose. I just don't."

"That's no explanation."

Mama makes a great show of picking at a thread on a buttonhole of her blouse while she thinks this over. "I guess the explanation is, I was proud of you," she says finally. "Proud of you for caring that much about a bald little girl. For acting from the heart for once instead of censoring yourself. I hoped you'd see the consequences weren't that bad, or at least that you'd think they were worth it. I knew they wouldn't actually lock you up. I figured it wouldn't hurt to leave you there for a while to contemplate your situation."

"Well, it was cruel."

"I know that now." Mama flinches at the word *cruel*, and right away I'm sorry I said it.

"Besides, how was I supposed to know you were proud of me?" I yell over the roar of the air conditioner. "When you didn't show up to get me, I thought you were ashamed. Throwing that basket was impulsive. You were always telling me not to be impulsive. Not to tell people about you-know-what."

"LilyRose, that was twenty years ago, and I've regretted it ever since. I just wanted you to use good judgment. I didn't want you talking about synesthesia to every Tom, Dick, and Harry, because not everybody understands. But I didn't want you to build a wall around yourself, either." She stops fiddling with her blouse, and her voice goes shaky. "I was misguided. I'm sorry."

I pretend I don't feel the sting of tears in my own eyes as I try to turn this into a joke. "Well, it's true, Mama. You *were* misguided." Mama looks astonished, then smiles. A second later we're both giggling and sobbing at the same time, and hugging and saying we're sorry. We don't even hear Jamene come in until she says, "Well, look here. I guess you two finally made up." As if her advice to ignore our differences instead of confronting them were not the reason for half of our problems!

"You ought to learn to knock," Mama says, but not very forcefully. After all these years, she knows Jamene won't.

"Mama, you need to lock your doors," I say. "Next time it could be someone even scarier than Jamene." We have this discussion often. Anyone could walk in and take every valuable Mama owns. Mama always says, "Oh LilyRose, you know I don't have anything valuable." This is not true.

"Sit down, both of you," Jamene commands as if she owns the house and we're the visitors. "I have something to tell you."

"Mama wants me to check the flowers before it gets too hot," I say. Jamene's "something to tell you" usually means gossip she's heard at the hairdresser's.

"Fine. Let's go check the flowers," she orders, which is odd because despite her olive skin that tans and never burns, Jamene hates the heat. She opens her skinny arms to herd us out. On the patio, it's quieter, away from the air conditioner, but even in the shade, the humid air feels like glue. Jamene is not about to venture down the stairs into the sunshine. She plops herself into one of the wrought iron chairs at the patio table, and motions us to do the same. Mama looks at me and shakes her head, just enough so Jamene won't notice, making me feel like the two of us are a team in cahoots against her, humoring her by sitting down.

"Okay, what's the big news?" I ask.

"It's about the story in the paper after you got arrested," Jamene says.

"That was over two weeks ago," Mama notes.

"Well, I didn't know this until last night, because Alex has been out of town so much," Jamene says testily. "If you don't want to hear, fine."

"Of course we do," Mama says.

"Well." Jamene pauses for effect. "LilyRose, you know why your story didn't run on the front page?"

"Why?"

"Because Alex talked them out of it."

"Huh," Mama says, in a tone that says she is not so sure.

"He did." Jamene pretends Mama is not there. "You remember how Alex left so quickly that night after you were arrested? Because he thought the paper might say something about Joey's baldness?"

"Not that baldness is exactly a secret," Mama defends.

"Well, it looked like he was just upset, and of course he *was*—no wonder. I was upset, too. But mainly he was lost in thought. Preoccupied because he was devising a plan. He always seems angry when he's doing that."

Mama shakes her head. Jamene pays no attention. "He went out so quickly because he wanted to get down to the newspaper office and speak with the editor before they put the paper to bed." She is so proud of her newspaper lingo—putting the paper to bed—that she pauses as if for applause.

"Newspapers don't usually print the names of minors," she goes on, "but there's no law that says they can't. It's purely an editorial decision. Alex went down there so the editor would know that even if he didn't print Joey's name, even if the story just said Bitsy had insulted a little bald girl, everyone in town would know who they were talking about."

"So he threatened to sue them?" I ask, recalling his legal prowess.

"Oh, I doubt it. I think he just convinced the editor it was the right thing to do. To tone down the story. Not to use too many details. Not to run it on page one," Jamene says. "So as not to embarrass Joey. Or you, either, for that matter."

"It sounds to me like I was just a by-product."

"If you don't get convicted, there's no story

for them anyway," Jamene says. "If you do—well, we'll see."

We'll see? I'm not sure exactly what this means. Probably nothing good.

At least Jamene's story explains Alex's odd behavior the night of my arrest and later at the post office, friendly one minute, icy the next. As long as I do my best to win my case, it's possible I'll help his daughter get through the summer without becoming a circus sideshow. If I plead guilty, everything Bitsy said will come out in court and end up in the next day's newspaper. No wonder Alex wants me to fight.

All this time Mama has been picking at the loose thread on her blouse. Now she yanks it out and stands up. "Well," she says, raising her eyebrows at me. "It miraculously appears that one of my tenants is a decent human being. Not a con man or a serial killer. Imagine that!"

She gives me goofy, wide-eyed look. I return it. It feels good to be friends.

Mama and Jamene retreat quickly into the cool house, leaving me to inspect the garden alone. Although Mama still refers to "Daddy's flowers" after all these years, most of them are mine. I plant the annuals each spring and tend them all summer, though not as carefully as I used to. Most of the zinnias are coated with powdery white mildew that's making the leaves shrivel, though the flowers still look bright and colorful, at least from a distance. Mildew doesn't often kill the plants. I'll spray them, and when it cools off a little, the new growth will look fine.

My hangover-dulled head is still pounding, but less fiercely than before. The sun must be burning the alcohol out of my system. My hair is pulled back into a ponytail, and the way it swings as I head for the storage shed and the spray bottles, it makes a little breeze against my neck. Even with the headache, I begin to remember how carefree I felt when I was twenty, tending to this yard with Daddy every Sunday it was warm.

I'm finished with the zinnias and about to spray the roses when I begin to feel I'm being watched. There's no one else in the yard. I look up at the kitchen window, expecting to see Mama or Jamene staring back, but they're not there. Then I raise my eyes toward the sun porch on the second floor. Sure enough, there's Alex, standing at one of the many windows, scowling down. At least I think he's scowling. Squinting against the brightness, it's hard to tell.

Under that disapproving glare, I want to wrap my arms around myself, hide the low V-neck of my tank top, pull a pair of slacks over my skimpy shorts. Then I tell myself, *get over it, LilyRose, there's no way a person can work outdoors in this heat except in a minimum of clothes*. For the briefest second I also think, thank goodness my legs tan so well. Then I censor that as ridiculous and inappropriate for an independent professional woman.

When I look up again, Alex is gone. The air feels emptier than before.

A moment later he's back, not in the window but standing right beside me as I aim the spray bottle at a rosebush about to be overtaken by blackspot. "I'm glad I ran into you," he says.

It's interesting, how he keeps telling me he's glad he ran into me when he's probably just the opposite. Today he's far more serious and preoccupied than he was at the post office, not exactly scowling but not jovial, either. "I'm glad to see you, too," I say, deciding to cheer him up. "Your mother-in-law told me this morning that you were even more the knight in shining armor than I knew. I wanted to thank you."

"Knight in shining armor?" He frowns.

"Not only did you come get me from the jail-house," I explain, "but I also reaped the benefits of your going to the newspaper to save Joey from the unwanted publicity I was about to foist on her." This sounds a little sour. I gentle my voice. "It's nice of you to go to all that trouble for your child. Not everyone would."

He regards me oddly, as if he's thinking, well, *most* parents would go to bat for their kid. What's the big deal? But what he says, in his melting russet voice, is, "I did it for you, too. Not just for Joey."

"For me?"

"It was the least I could do. You seemed pretty upset that day."

"I did?"

"Oh, yes, ma'am."

Inwardly groaning, I picture how I must have looked to him. "Lord, I must have been a sorry sight."

"Only relatively sorry. Besides, I know how much you hate your mother taking in tenants. I would have felt responsible if you lost your house and business and had to move in with her."

"Who told you I hate her taking in tenants?"

"Jamene. Who else?"

Both of us smile. Both of us squint. It's insanely sunny, especially if you're trying to deal with the after-effects of too much wine. I have a bizarre yearning to move forward into the coolness of Alex's shadow.

"You look hot," he says, reading my mind. "Come sit down. I want to ask you a favor."

A *favor?* Carrying the spray bottle, I lead him down the path toward the storage shed, where a concrete bench, littered with small gardening tools, is shaded by a cherry tree. "I know Joey's been coming to your store," he says when we've moved enough of the implements to sit. "I hope she isn't driving you crazy."

"Not at all. I told you before, she's pretty talented. She's actually a big help." I don't say how surprised I am he hasn't forbidden me to have her there.

"She certainly seems to enjoy it."

"And vice versa."

He stares into the middle distance for a moment, during which time I note that he has a lot of hair on his arms, which, despite his lean physique, look remarkably muscular. "You wanted a favor?" I ask.

"Oh, yes." The grim expression again. "It's about Joey's hair."

"Of which there is still not a great deal," I remind him.

"Not yet." It occurs to me that Jamene is right about Alex looking angry when he's lost in thought. Maybe it's nothing personal.

He clears his throat. I pick up a trowel lying beside me on the bench and attempt to twirl it in my fingers like a baton.

"I know you talk—you and Joey—while she's in your store," he says.

"Sometimes." I see that twirling a trowel is not actually possible, given the size of my fingers. I make myself stop.

"I know on the surface she seems tough, not your typical flighty adolescent."

"She's very bright," I say. "Very self-confident."

"Not as confident as people think. Underneath the bravado, she's pretty sensitive." He rubs his shoulder, the one that sits a little higher than the other. "I don't think she's ever told anyone the real reason she shaved her head. I think whatever it is, it's still bothering her." Casually, as if he's been practicing, he asks, "Has she told you anything about it?"

"Only that she didn't want to have to go with her mother to England."

"Did you believe it?"

"No."

"Neither do I. But…well, she likes you. If you keep at it, talk to her a little more, maybe she'll tell you what's really on her mind." He pushes his glasses up on his sweaty nose. "Would you mind?"

"Of course not. I'm flattered you asked." Lifting the trowel in my hand, I add, "I'll keep digging."

He groans at the pun. "Thanks."

I'm about to get up, but Alex stays seated and massages his shoulder a little more energetically. "So Joey's really helpful?" he asks, suddenly a typical concerned parent, anxious for news about his child.

"Oh, yes!" I say. "She's very creative. We don't always put the gifts in baskets. We like to use all kinds of containers to fit the theme—like a pretty baking dish for a housewarming. Last week Joey had the idea of using a turned-over child's umbrella for a bridal shower. It was just the right size, and everyone loved it." I feel a smile spreading across my face as I remember something else. "Sometimes she's *too* creative." The words are out before I can censor them. Alex looks alarmed.

"Too creative?"

"Oh, nothing bad! The other day she brought in

a piece of hollowed-out old log she'd found. She was so excited. It was beautiful, really. Gray and weathered, with a perfect oval for putting things in. But it would have been impossible to get clean. The health department would have put me out of business in a heartbeat if I'd put anything edible inside. I felt terrible telling her."

"Oh." Alex looks so relieved that for the first time I forget that he's a tenant, forget I'm unwillingly indebted to him, forget everything except how vulnerable he is—a quality that touches a soft spot in me I didn't even know I had.

We head back to the house in the blazing sunlight, in heat so intense I wouldn't be surprised if I caught on fire before I reached the rose trellis—LilyRose Sheffield, Victim of Spontaneous Combustion—but somehow I don't.

Inside, Mama is just coming down the stairs in a floaty summer dress I've never seen, ready to go to church. When she asks me to come back for dinner, I accept.

CHAPTER 11

Zee sets the table in the dining room because of the heat, though she cooks the chicken outside on the grill. She prepares everything else in the noisy air-conditioned kitchen, including the squash casserole from Jamene's oversupply of summer crooknecks. She hopes Alex will forgive her for the casserole. It's only a side dish. There's also coleslaw, baked beans and fruit salad for him to choose from. It's a picnic meal, even though she's serving it inside on good dishes.

For the first time in ages, the dining room won't feel empty. As tenants, Alex and Leona Richie are almost always there, of course, but tonight, when Jamene and Joey and Kent and LilyRose arrive, there will be seven of them altogether. Zee loves having a crowd in her dining room. She loves her dining room, period. She loves the solid feel of the huge mahogany table that once belonged to Cy's grandmother, a big clunky thing with oversized clawed feet. She feels the same way about the massive cherry settee Zee's great aunt handed down. The chairs come from all over, from Aunt Rose and Cy's cousin Melba and two or three others. She had them all upholstered in the same plum-colored fabric so they'd look like they belong together, but they don't. Some have curved legs and some straight, and the backs of the chairs aren't all the same height. She doesn't know what styles they are. She doesn't know the first thing about furniture styles. But she loves each one of her fourteen chairs, as if each were a priceless, one-of-a-kind antique— which, for all she knows, maybe it is. The dishes and glasses are mismatched, too, though to Zee's way of thinking, when they are placed on a tablecloth for a festive meal, they have a kind of symmetry. Some came from relatives she never knew, dead before she was born, and others from Cy's side of the family or from her own distant aunts and cousins she didn't see often enough to put a face with a name. Zee loves that each of these people left her something, even though they might not have known at the time she'd end up with it. Just the fact that they cared enough to hand down their furniture means a lot to her, and in an odd way, she feels it means something to them, too. Whenever Zee seats more than six people in her dining room, she feels like all the ancestors are looking on with approval, down through the generations further than anyone can remember.

Aside from seeing everyone in her favorite surroundings, the best thing about this particular evening is LilyRose's being in such a good mood from start to finish. She comes in showered and fresh, in cropped white slacks and a stretchy purple top that sets off the little bit of sunburn she got on her face this morning in the garden. She's pretty from head to toe, her hair shiny the way it gets when it's just been washed, and her strappy white sandals revealing her tanned arches and the new French pedicure on her toes. LilyRose always did have pretty feet.

LilyRose offers to help Zee, and when Zee takes her up on it, LilyRose is Miss Busy Bee herself. She carries platters from kitchen to dining room. She gets the chicken off the grill with a serving fork. At Zee's prodding, she tastes one of the drumsticks to see if it's done, and is in such high spirits that she even leans close to Zee and says with a laugh,

"Mama, the curlicues in this chicken need to be unwound." This is the kind of statement LilyRose would usually censor altogether unless they were alone, something that wouldn't escape her lips for fear that someone else might hear.

Zee used to think LilyRose was talking in code when she said things like curlicues needing to be unwound, but now she thinks she understands. When they begin the meal, Zee realizes the chicken is a little bit tough. Zee doesn't have any sense of curlicues, herself, but she can imagine them, stringy pieces of chicken-flesh all loose and flaccid when the meat is raw, then getting tighter and tighter as the flesh cooks through, and finally too tight if it's not removed from the heat on time.

At least Zee *thinks* this is what LilyRose is experiencing. She's always aware that she doesn't really know. Does LilyRose *taste* these curlicues, or do they appear before her eyes the way columns of glass do when she drinks lemonade? Maybe it's a combination—seeing the curlicues the way she sees pink when she eats angel food cake, and also tasting them in her mouth. This is a confusing concept to Zee, no matter how long she dwells on it, and in spite of all the articles she's read over the years. One person can never tell exactly what's in another person's head, even someone close to you. This knowledge makes her a little sad. She understands synesthesia, and she doesn't. But if LilyRose could always be as carefree as she is tonight, Zee wouldn't care.

She knows part of the reason LilyRose is happy is that Joey is showering her with worshipful attention. Alex is looking at her, too, and LilyRose knows it. More specifically, Alex is looking at LilyRose's cleavage, which is visible above the plunging, purple neckline of her body-hugging top. Zee's parental bias notwithstanding, it looks marvelous. Cleavage, Zee has always believed, can be a powerful tool in the war between the sexes.

All the same, as glad as Zee is to see this cessation of hostilities between her tenant and her daughter, she knows it doesn't mean anything. Flirting is a game LilyRose has liked to play since she first developed curves, a game Zee frowned on at first until she realized LilyRose was in control of it and not vice versa. There were times when LilyRose went through boyfriends like a bee through springtime flowers. Except for Jeremy Taylor, there were no episodes of unbridled foolishness. It is not always a bad thing to be a flirt. In recent years, Zee has actually wished LilyRose would practice her skills more often, at least until she finds the person to spend her life with, the person that so far she doesn't even think she wants.

"Delicious, as usual," Kent says, spooning another serving of fruit salad onto his plate. In the short-sleeved blue shirt that matches his eyes, he looks almost handsome, although no one would ever call him that. Maybe he just looks handsome to Zee. He turns to LilyRose.

"I'm sorry about your arrest. I know you've worked hard to get where you are."

"Don't remind me," LilyRose groans, but it is not a serious groan; it is a good-natured, I-can't-believe-this-happened-to me groan. "I've been working on my career for twelve years, and for all I know, it's about to come to a screeching halt in a couple of weeks." She glances at Alex and then quickly looks away, as if she's saying to him, my career is all that's important to me, at the same time that her chest is sticking out of that tight top.

"Well, try not to worry," Kent says. "I was arrested at about your same age. I'd been working on my career, too. And here I am to tell the tale."

"You were arrested?"

"At the office Christmas party in the banquet room of a fancy restaurant, with my boss and all my colleagues looking on. Someone told me I looked like a Munchkin in *The Wizard of Oz*. It wasn't the first time I'd heard that, but it was the first time after three glasses of Kentucky Knockout Punch. I took offense and took the guy down. I'd been a wrestler in high school. He got up and I took him down again. I pinned him and then smacked him in the face. Let's just say I was hard to restrain. I spent the night in jail and was fired on Monday morning."

"You were fired?" LilyRose's eyebrows shoot up in surprise.

"Best thing that ever happened to me. At the next company I went to work for, they told me they liked an employee to be assertive."

Joey giggles. Kent winks at her. "Remember what Kermit the Frog said about being green? It's not easy being short, either." To LilyRose he says, "You'll survive it. Better than you think."

"I plan to," LilyRose says, and she sounds like she believes it.

Zee is so grateful to Kent that she doesn't even care if his story is true. She's pretty sure it isn't.

The evening progresses smoothly all through

dinner, like someone put on exactly the right music and everything is harmonizing just the way it should. Afterward, LilyRose says she'll help Zee clean up. She shoos Alex and Kent and Joey into the yard to throw a ball around, and tells Jamene and Mrs. Richie to go out to the patio to watch. Zee thinks, *it is so nice of her to do this*. Then the door closes and they are alone in the kitchen and LilyRose puts her hands on her hips.

"What's going on with Kent, Mama? He's a nice man, but he's not your boarder anymore. I know you're feeding him at least a couple of times a week."

"Well, why shouldn't I, honey?" Zee asks, which is a perfectly logical question, considering it's her house and her food. There's no reason her heart should be thudding in her chest the way it's doing, so hard she's afraid LilyRose will hear it.

"Food costs money, Mama. It's a major expense in an operation like this. If you really consider yourself a business person the way you say you do, you have to take that into account."

"Well, I have taken it into account," Zee says. "I've thought about it long and hard. And that's exactly why Kent is here." She is making this up as she goes along. "He likes the meals I serve. He has his own place now, but he doesn't cook. So he pays me to make him supper." She is surprised how easily these words have come to her lips.

LilyRose narrows her eyes. Then the tension drains from her face, and she laughs. "I swear, Mama, a year from now you'll be running a regular restaurant." Zee can tell she's impressed. This is all the more reason for Zee to feel ashamed of her lie, but she doesn't. She turns to the sink and starts to rinse the dishes.

Between the whoosh of water and the whoosh of the air conditioner, it's hard to talk, so they just work for a while, which is a relief because it gives Zee time to think. This is the first time she has lied to LilyRose outright like this. She supposes you could argue that it was a lie when she told LilyRose she wouldn't take in male boarders, but Zee doesn't think so. The question of male boarders was an uncertainty. The question of Kent is not. Kent is not paying for the meals he eats here. Zee wouldn't hear of it. Her statement that this is a business arrangement is an out-and-out untruth. But Zee knows it's an explanation LilyRose will accept. Zee can't tell her the rest right now, not that she's "seeing" Kent and certainly not that Kent has started spending whole nights here, leaving early enough that no one will know. And she certainly can't tell her they have—well, a relationship, though the physical part of it so far is strictly above the waist.

Above the waist. The words make Zee feel like she's about fourteen. They are certainly not words a mother can utter to her daughter.

Carrying another huge armload of platters and dishes in from the dining room, LilyRose sets them on the counter. "Honestly, Mama," she says. "I think you used up every bit of your china for this meal and then borrowed some of Jamene's."

"And went to the dollar store, too, for a few extra pots and pans."

LilyRose rolls her eyes. Much as Zee hates lying to her daughter about Kent, much as it puts a little niggle of worry and foreboding at the back of her mind, she can't help but smile at the idea that LilyRose is joking with her as if nothing at all has changed for either of them these past few weeks. She just can't get into lengthy explanations right now. There's no point in it. They are having too good a time.

CHAPTER 12

Like everyone else in town, I'm relieved when a wild, crackling thunderstorm finally signals a break in the weather. It's still hot, as it always is at this time of year, but the humidity is down, and there's a freshness to the air that makes it more breathable than it's been in weeks. It's so nice outside that Bitsy Eversole gives up her sling and her early-morning tennis games at the club in order to play at her regular time in the afternoon. Her desire to say her serving arm will never be the same has been quashed by her yearning for competitive sport! I suspect she'll be up to some other kind of trickery before it's all over, but for the moment, I'm pleased. I'd be even more pleased if my court date hadn't been moved from the original difficult week with two major jobs due, to the week right before the band concert and barbecue, which is likely to be my busiest of the season. In the back of my mind I keep trying to figure out how to take off a day to go to court while still getting everything ready for the big weekend.

But mainly, right now, it's the week of Joey's hair. Or rather, it's the week of the twenty or thirty accounts Joey gives about why she shaved it. I try to be subtle when I bring up the subject, but she is onto me. Making up new explanations is a game, apparently as much fun for her as it once was to invent reasons why she needed to grow up to be a cheetah. She's as good at it as she is at Sudoku.

"I've told you before," she says on the first day, starting with the simple, tried-and-true story no one believes. "I shaved my head because I knew my mom wouldn't take a bald child to Europe."

"And I've told *you* before," I laugh, "that your mom would be just as proud of you bald as with a full head of hair. Not to mention that Jamene would pitch a fit if your mom took you to Europe instead of sending you to Fern Hollow for the summer. Your visits are the highlight of her year."

After that, Joey's explanations grow ever more far-fetched and bold. She had gotten gum in her hair and tried to cut it out. She cut too much, cut some more to even it out and pretty soon made such a mess that she shaved it.

"Unlikely," I say.

She shrugs and casually changes her story. "Actually, it was because of the ticks," she intones gravely. "I didn't want to tell anybody because I thought they'd be too grossed out. My friend Olivia and I took her dog into the woods, and I got three of them in my hair. Three! They were walking all over my head and making it itch like crazy. A thing like that would make you shave your head, too."

"Are you and Olivia actually *allowed* to go into the woods?" I ask.

"Well, maybe not," Joey admits.

By the next day she has invented an epidemic of head lice at school, complete with an evil nurse armed with metal combs. "It was awful," she moans. "You had to stand in line in front of her, and when it was your turn, you had to look down at the floor while she parted your hair and checked your scalp. She wasn't gentle, either. She'd tug at your tangles like you were numb. One girl actually cried. I decided I'd rather be bald than face her. Even if I *had* lice, I wasn't about to put that goo in my hair that you have to use to get rid of them."

Alex laughs when I tell him this one. "I haven't heard anything about lice in school since she went to kindergarten." He's taken to calling me each evening after work to get my report, and—to my surprise—I've taken to looking forward to our conversations. We always begin with Joey, but then we veer off into subjects ranging from computer viruses to the unfortunate timing of my court date, so close to the big barbecue/band concert in the park. "You'll be ready for it," he assures me. "Joey will help. I'll help you myself, if you'll let me. I'll stand at your booth and sell cookies."

"Not necessary. Angela will be there, and also Bonnie O'Dell, who owned the store before I did. She's making most of the desserts we're going to sell, and she's going to work at the booth all day."

"So you're rejecting my application?"

"If I lose my case, no one will want to buy anything from me, anyway. I'll be a pariah."

"You're not going to lose. I'll come by early and help you set up."

His offer comes so naturally that it's easy to accept. I begin to feel, as I have a few times before, that Alex is someone I'd like to have as a friend. Considering our mutual concern for Joey, maybe we *are* friends. It's been a long time since I've had someone to talk with like this. I have to be so vigilant about what I say that it's usually easier not to start anything. One word about throwing out a batch of petits fours because they tasted as gray as warmed-over mashed potatoes, and that would be that. It wouldn't be any different with Alex. He's too concerned about wanting Joey to be normal ever to trust someone who isn't.

All the same, I'm enjoying this while it lasts—which, if I'm lucky, might be until the end of the summer when he and Joey both return home. Sheltered by the benign phone waves, I'm unlikely to precipitate one of Alex's rapid-fire changes of mood. And it's comforting to talk to him from this distance, away from his disturbing *nearness* and those unbidden twists of desire. I let myself relax even though I know a firelight-in-fall kind of voice like this, russet and gold, can be so warm and mellow that it mesmerizes you even in the middle of summer.

"Has Joey told you about Locks of Love?" Alex asks.

"Locks of Love?"

"It's a charity. Girls and women grow their hair to a certain length and then have it cut to make wigs for children with a disease called alopecia that leaves them without any hair. Joey had most of her hair cut off not long before she shaved her head. At first I thought she shaved it on an impulse because she hated the new short style. Then she came up with the story about Stephanie not wanting to take a bald child to Europe, and I figured there was something else going on. I doubt Locks of Love has anything to do with it, but I thought she might mention it."

"Not so far." Then I remember that she did. She told me last summer that she was going to let it grow all winter. I think ten or twelve inches was required for a wig. The fact that she hasn't said a word about it now seems odd, since we talk about everything else. I don't say this to Alex.

By the end of the week, Joey still hasn't mentioned Locks of Love, and I'm reluctant to bring it up, partly because growing hair for charity sounds serious, and we are in a distinctly un-serious mood. Joey has progressed from goofy, harebrained stories to truly outlandish ones, and both of us are having fun. Also—I hate to admit this—the sillier her stories are, the more I enjoy relating them to Alex. I caution myself not to use Joey to get attention from her father. I hope it hasn't come to that. I won't let it.

"If I tell you the absolute truth," Joey says on Friday, in a stage whisper which is completely unnecessary because Angela is out to lunch and the shop is empty. "If I tell you the absolute truth, will you promise not to tell Daddy or Grandma yet? Promise you'll let me tell them myself?"

There is such a note of heartfelt drama in her voice that my heart gives a little leap. "Sure."

"Cross your heart and hope to die?"

This is a phrase I thought she gave up years ago, but I go along and cross my heart.

"Okay," she says. "I shaved my head because I'm a lesbian." She impales me with her sternest glare. "I wanted to look a little more butch."

Butch? It's all I can do to keep a straight face. Even bald, Joey is anything but "butch." Her girly-girl earrings glimmer in her ears. Today's T-shirt is a vibrant pink, her signature color. Her flip-flops are magenta. I force my hands to keep braiding long strips of bubblegum into strands of curling ribbon for a gift basket, and freeze my neutral expression into place. "You're sure about this? You don't feel it might be too soon to know?"

"Oh, I know, all right."

"How?"

"Kathleen Sloan," she whispers.

I nod. If Joey's story made any sense at all, Katie Sloan would certainly be a suitable love object. But there are discrepancies. First, Joey shaved her head before she arrived in Fern Hollow and saw Katie for the first time. Second, I'm almost certain Joey has observed Katie only from afar, as she shoots baskets in her driveway down the street. At thirteen, Katie is already a great beauty, tall and raven-haired, with gold-flecked eyes, a pouty mouth and astonishingly long legs. She's also a sweet girl, more athlete than vamp, a bit confused by the touch of Venus that has overtaken her while she's still so young. All of this only adds to her allure. On any given evening, three or four teen-aged boys can be seen walking by her house or circling the block on bikes, inventing reasons to catch a glimpse of her.

Despite the slew of young people, both male and female, who are either smitten with Katie or jealous of her, somehow I think that Joey finds her more an object of convenience than infatuation. In any case, the topic calls for delicacy. In my softest, most confessional tone, I say, "When I was your age, I was in love with Paula Wise."

This stops Joey cold, but just for a moment. She wrinkles her nose. "Paula Wise? You mean the lady who works at the farmers' market? Who wears sleeveless blouses and doesn't shave under her arms?"

"The very same."

"Yuk."

"I don't think she had hair under her arms back then. Probably not old enough for secondary sex characteristics."

Joey snickers.

"Girls your age often have crushes on other girls," I say earnestly. "Which doesn't necessarily mean they don't like boys. The year after Paula, I was in love with Johnny Brannon and then Larry Eng."

"Maybe you were bisexual." She pronounces the word with great authority.

"No." I shake my head and examine my bubble-gum string. "After Paula it was all males."

Looking up from the bow she's working on, Joey opens her mouth, pauses, then seems to gather the courage to rush on. "But you never got married. Maybe you were right the first time. Maybe disgusting Mrs. Wise was your true love."

I try not to roll my eyes or make a comic face. "My point is, you'll know more later."

"Some people know practically from birth," she informs me, her tone so professorial that I'm sure this is a fact she gleaned from research. "I'll tell Daddy and Grandma this weekend. I'm going to be completely out of the closet about this."

"I see."

"It's liberating"—another word she enunciates in such a way that it sounds like she's quoting. "Once I tell the world, you won't have to go around assaulting people to protect me."

"Well, that's comforting." I snap the bubble-gum braid in her direction. She giggles and darts away, then stops and grows serious. "You should come out of the closet with your own secret," she says.

"Oh? What secret is that?"

"Synesthesia."

Dumbstruck, I set the braid onto the work table and stare at her.

"Don't look so shocked. I heard my grandmother talking about it with your mother."

"You did?" I thought Mama and Jamene would be more discreet.

"Don't worry, they didn't know I was there. They weren't snitching on you or anything."

"Ah. So it was you doing the snitching."

"Spying," Joey corrects, unashamed.

"And who else knows?" I ask in a voice that trembles more than I mean it to.

"Nobody. I wouldn't tell Roberto. You can't trust boys. I didn't even tell Daddy."

"Well. Good." The bubble-gum braid is going to be the handle of a small basket that will hold prizes for a children's party. I begin tying it in place, clinging to it as if to a life raft.

"I mean, really," Joey says. "You act like you think I can't keep a secret. Which, obviously, I can."

"Obviously."

"What I want to know is—" she pushes the bow aside and regards me eagerly "—what it's *like*. Are you one of those synesthesia people who see letters in color? I read an article about it. Every time they see an A, say, it always looks blue to them. Or orange for B. It's kind of amazing. Does that happen to you?"

"I hate to disappoint you, but no, I don't see letters in color."

Joey is unfazed. "But you *taste* colors? Your

mother said when you eat angel food cake, it tastes pink."

Do I really want to discuss this after all these years of keeping silent? I hesitate, then say, "Well, yes."

"That must be so awesome!" She's so excited that it's hard to be upset with her, just for being observant and smart.

"It's awesome except when people find out about it and think you're crazy," I caution.

"Nobody thinks you're crazy!"

"Oh, you'd be surprised."

"Why would anyone think it's crazy? It's more like being able to do something neat. Like twist your legs behind your back. Or hold your breath a long time under water, like that guy on TV."

"Oh, I see. Like being a freak." For once, I'm talking about my personal freakdom with a smile on my face.

"No!" Joey protests. "It's more like— Well, I'm not sure. For me, knowing a person with a rare linking of senses…" she's quoting again "…is like… It's like knowing a movie star!"

This makes absolutely no sense, but she says it with such assurance that I have to laugh.

"Since I found out about it anyway, you can tell me about it, right?" she asks. "I want to know everything."

"Everything might take a while."

"Who cares?" Joey gestures to the work table. "We've got all day."

"We've got half an hour," I tell her. "Until Angela comes back from lunch. This is a secret, remember?"

Joey beams.

But for the rest of the day, Angela is in the back of the shop or out running errands so much that I do tell Joey "everything," more or less. Every detail fascinates her. She's right that being out is liberating. I talk and talk, my relief undiminished by the fact that I'm out only to a single twelve-year-old. It will be especially liberating if she keeps mum about it, as she promises.

That evening I'm in the shower when the phone rings. I know it's Alex. In the euphoria that's followed my outing to Joey, I'm full of energy, tempted to grab a towel and run to pick it up. Then a quick shiver runs through me in spite of the hot water, and it occurs to me that there's nothing I can say to him. I certainly can't tell him about Joey's dis-

covery of my synesthesia—and, it strikes me suddenly, I can't tell him her lesbian story, either. In retrospect, the tale seems part of an increasingly
desperate effort to distract me and make me laugh—
anything to keep me from getting closer to the real
reason she shaved her head, which she wants so
badly to protect. She doesn't want to be out about
her baldness. She wants to hide it behind layers of
comic lies. Much as I want to talk to Alex—and I
want to talk to him very much—I feel a need to
protect him from her confession of homosexuality,
and to protect Joey, too. Besides being patently
untrue, the story seems too sad, too delicate, too—
well, sexual—to reveal to her father. Both of them
would be miserable if they knew the other knew. I
picture Alex's warm hazel eyes behind the glasses,
turning from amused to troubled in that quicksilver
way of his, and then from troubled to angry—not at
me, not at Joey, but at himself for not being able to
understand her, help her, ease her way. If only from
a distance, I begin to appreciate the powerful misery
of parental helplessness. And there's nothing I can
do about it, except to keep a little of the hurt at bay.
I am afraid to talk to Alex because I'm afraid of
what I'd say.

Turning off the shower, I know what I'm going to do. I change clothes, pick up the ads that came in the morning paper, and rush out to spend a long, long evening shopping, alone, at the mall. Just so I won't be tempted, I leave my cell phone at home.

This is the night I have the dream. I'm alone at first, reaching up through darkness toward sheets of translucent, pastel lights that billow and flutter like garments on a clothesline. I think this is what the aurora borealis must look like, but Fern Hollow is so far removed from the northern lights that I can't be sure. The colors remind me of the ones that float across my vision with certain sounds or certain tastes, yet more substantial, somehow. They are so beautiful that I hold out my arms, wanting to touch them.

After a time, Alex is there, too, his glasses a little crooked on his face, his shoulder askew. We stand together like old friends, not speaking, watching the ribbons of light with wonder, aware that they're just a little too far away to touch.

It's all very pleasant, lingering there, watching the colors dance and flutter just above our heads. I could stay this way for a long time.

Then at the edge of my vision I catch a glimpse

of Alex's profile, the earpiece of his old-fashioned glasses reinforced with masking tape—and without warning the honeyed glow of friendship tightens into something more urgent, part yearning and part pleasure, threading through my belly like a promise.

I awaken with a start. The only light in the room is from my digital alarm clock, which reads 3:07. I'm sweating, though the air-conditioning is purring and the ceiling fan is on. I know at once that I must have dreamed about the bands of color because Joey and I talked about color so much when I was telling her about synesthesia. Probably I dreamed about Alex because there's so much I've kept from him today. That would make sense.

But that ripple of desire?

This is a man who might be a friend at the moment, but whose interest in me is limited to my ability to help protect his daughter. A man whose attitude toward me sometimes turns to active dislike, and who would probably feel real revulsion if he knew the woman trying to help Joey through the temporary oddity of baldness is stuck with her own, permanent oddity of synesthesia. Nor do I think it would please him to discover I'm in cahoots with Joey to make sure he doesn't find out.

What makes no sense to me, knowing all this, is that my body doesn't seem to care.

All I know is that talking to Alex on the phone, from a distance—or not talking to him at all— doesn't protect me from these annoying losses of control, so agreeable in the moment, so dangerous in retrospect. This is not like me. And what *that* means, I have no idea.

CHAPTER 13

"It looks like we're going to have company," Angela says as I walk into the back door of the store on Monday morning.

"Company?"

She beckons me to follow her through the shop, and points out the storefront window. Although it's only nine-fifty and the businesses on Main Street open at ten, there's already a line of SUVs and luxury cars parked at the curbs—Volvos and BMWs, a Lexus or two. This is unusual at any time, but especially on a Monday morning. As if at a signal, the car doors open and well-dressed women, probably a dozen of them, begin to emerge.

"Oh, no," I say, though I'm not sure yet exactly what's happening, only that it can't be good. I might be looking through a time warp, except that I recognize most of the women as the local country-club set. Some are a bit younger than I am, some as much as ten years older, but all of them are dressed as if they'd chosen their outfits fifty or sixty years ago, in preparation for some important ladies' church function. Not a single one is wearing slacks. To a woman, they are dressed in pastel summer dresses and pumps with three-inch heels. Not espadrilles, not platform sandals. Just high-heeled pumps. Some carry pastel purses over their arms—no shoulder bags—the sort Mama used to have for church. A few even wear colorful, wide-brimmed hats like the ones department stores sell in the weeks before Easter. Hats!

Emerging from their cars, the women smooth their skirts and walk daintily around to open their trunks. They take out placards attached to long sticks. My heart flutters as the first one is lifted. Boycott The Bopper, it reads.

Well, of course.

LilyRose Sheffield, Bopper.

Bitsy Eversole appears in the crowd with a stack of flyers on fluorescent yellow paper. Even without seeing them up close, I know what they say—that the proprietor of Bountiful Baskets knowingly and willingly bopped her with a gift basket, causing her shoulder irreparable harm, and should be boycotted from now until kingdom come.

"It's a picket line," Angela whispers.

"So I see." It occurs to me then that the women with hats brought them to protect themselves from the sun while demonstrating in front of my store. Not to be intimidated, I march to the front door and turn the Closed sign to Open.

Usually sales are slow at ten in the morning, so it's not as if Bitsy is warding off a big rush. Angela and I both act as if it's business as usual, but only because we can't think of anything else to do. Angela occupies herself with a stack of bills while I turn to a bunch of small bows I mean to use on the mini-baskets for the band concert. Neither of us actually does any work. Angela flips through the papers but doesn't make out a single check. I fool with the ribbon but don't complete a single bow. We are too aware of the scene outside, where the women march in a silent oval up and down the sidewalk in front of the store, holding their placards aloft. There are only a few passers-by at this hour, but Bitsy makes sure each of them gets a flyer.

Fifteen minutes later, I get another surprise. Making her way through the picket line toward the shop is my old high school buddy, Dorrie Sizemore, holding her little girl (first child, only daughter) by one hand, and clutching Bitsy's flyer and a shopping list in the other.

I can't say that Dorrie and I have remained close. She was, after all, the one who got me assigned to the school's drug program on the day of my raspberry sherbet experience all those years ago. I eventually forgave her—synesthesia is a hard concept to grasp, after all—but it goes without saying that I never confided in her again. We still phone one another occasionally, even though she's as busy with the care of three small children as I am with my career. Sometimes I think we keep in touch mainly because it's a habit neither of us is brave enough to break.

All the same, this morning I'm awfully glad to see her. Her shoulders are squared. She looks defiant. Her cropped jeans and wedged sandals seem just the right attire for a summer day in the twenty-first century.

"Dorrie! You just walked through a picket line!"

"Don't I know it." Dorrie grins. To her daughter she says, "Sit down on that bench a minute, Kristi, honey, and have one of those pretty cookies—" pointing to one of Bonnie O'Dell's red-white-and-blue sugar cookies, which I immediately dispense. "I heard about this—" Dorrie points out the door "—and I decided it was time to buy everything I've been meaning to buy all summer." She hands me the list, which is substantial.

"You heard about this? How come I didn't?"

"You don't live next door to Ginny Evans," she says, naming Bitsy's doubles partner from the club. "I would have called to warn you except that I just got the news." She hands the cookie to her daughter. "Say thank you, Kristi," and the little girl does.

"What about your other kids? Where did you leave them on such short notice?"

"My mom." Dorrie leans across the counter. "Any enemy of Bitsy Eversole," she whispers conspiratorially, "is a friend of mine." She hands me the flyer, which turns out to say pretty much what I thought it would, and maybe a little bit more.

When I finish reading, Dorrie stabs a finger in the direction of the picketers on the street. "Is this legal?"

"I guess it must be."

"But you're not sure?"

"Well, no."

"Not that it's any of my business, but I'd find

out this minute, if it were me." Dorrie sounds as wrought-up as she did the day she went blubbering to the guidance counselor, although this time I find myself grateful instead of mortified. "Speaking of finding out—" she says.

Outside, as it does most mornings, a Fern Hollow police cruiser inches up Main Street on its downtown patrol. It doesn't brake as it approaches the picketers.

"Why isn't he stopping?" Dorrie demands.

"I'll go ask!" Angela exclaims, and rushes out of the store, through the picket line, and into the middle of the street to flag down the cruiser. A few of the women snicker as Angela raises both hands above her head and waves wildly, allowing the sleeves of her baggy blouse to ride up and flap against her arms like wings.

Finally, the police car comes to a halt. The passenger side window rolls down, and Angela rushes over, speaking into the car with many gestures toward the picket line and the store. When she finishes, the door opens slowly. In one measured, leisurely motion, the bulky, uniformed figure of Dinky Lopak gets out. Just our luck that he's on duty today. None of the picketers look at him or say a word. I think this is a general rule of picketing—eyes front, mouth shut—though I can't say from firsthand experience. Angela practically drags Dinky into the store.

Dorrie doesn't wait for me to speak. "Does the town actually allow this?" she demands. "Does it let people march in front of any store they want and call somebody names just because they feel like it?"

Very deliberately, Dinky turns his back to me—police officer not deigning to address criminal—and says to Dorrie with dripping politeness, "Mrs. Eversole did get hit with a gift basket."

Dorrie's eyes flash. "She got hit, yes, but that doesn't mean anybody 'bopped' her. Does LilyRose Sheffield strike you as somebody who would assault her own customer?"

Based on our trip-to-the-jailhouse conversation, I know Dinky would like to utter a resounding *yes*. Instead, with admirable meekness, he tells Dorrie, "They do have a permit, ma'am."

Ma'am. As if Dorrie were old enough to be his mother.

Dorrie's daughter, Kristi, stops munching her cookie and stares wide-eyed at the gun holster at Dinky's waist. I step in front of him to block her view of the weapon, giving Dinky no choice but to look me in the eye.

"Well, thanks for clearing this up," I tell him, as if the two of us were the ones having this conversation. The aftershave I remember from the day of my arrest assaults my nostrils with the scent of ersatz cinnamon. I motion toward the door to indicate he's welcome to leave.

Dinky looks confused. Then, aware of the audience outside, he regains his composure and saunters out. It occurs to me that, if one of the Eversoles asked for it, the police department would issue a permit for anything from a bake sale to a gathering of white supremacist skinheads, no questions asked.

Which doesn't necessarily mean it's the right thing to do.

Dorrie and I raise our eyebrows at each other. "And what about *this?*" She slaps at the flyer lying on the counter. Little Kristi holds her forgotten cookie in her hand and regards her mother with alarm. I shrug, deciding it's time to call my lawyer, but not until Dorrie leaves.

"I can't tell you how much I appreciate this," I say. "Not many people would come down here just to show they're not afraid to cross a picket line."

"Oh, I enjoyed it," Dorrie says, and looks like she means it. I fill her order, give her a twenty percent discount, and send her off with a bag of goodies that will put all three of her children on a sugar-high for a week. I'm about to pick up the phone and dial Carolyn when Angela, still peering out the window at the picketers, says, "I can hardly believe this. Those *costumes*. It looks like the 1960s all over again."

Well, of course!

"That's it exactly!" I tell her. "Remember the picketers from the civil rights movement? This is how they dressed. In church clothes. Hats. Even gloves. Very respectable. I think Bitsy wants to remind me of that."

"What on earth for?" Angela asks.

"Back in high school we were both finalists in an essay contest about the civil rights movement, and I won. I think she's held it against me ever since."

"For twenty years?"

"I know. It seems ridiculous," I agree. But by now I'm sure this parody of a civil rights demonstration is only partly about Bitsy wanting to conjure up a sympathetic image of respectable people with right on their side, a week before my trial. Mostly, it's to remind me it doesn't matter who got the medal for a silly essay twenty years ago. It's Bitsy's way of saying, Look! I'm the winner, and you're the loser, after all. Childish, yes. But pure Bitsy. I think my throwing the basket at her gave her an unexpected chance for revenge. Sure, she expects to win in court next week and make a laughingstock out of me, but she's clever enough to hedge her bets. If she doesn't win, at least she'll have *this*.

A moment later, as if Bitsy's read my thoughts and decided she's made her point, the picket line begins to break up. Into the trunks go the placards. Into the cars go the protestors, including Bitsy herself in a lemon-yellow shirtwaist and matching shoes. The line of cars drives off. Having done their civic duty, the ladies of the country club are probably heading out to lunch.

Oh, this is Bitsy's talent, even more than tennis! Play-acting and posturing at someone else's expense. Giggling over a practical joke with her little sorority of followers. This is not about personal injury, and it's not about principles. It's not even about boycotting the store. It's about showing the world who has lots of friends and who doesn't. All with a smile on her face.

Fury creeps up my neck like a spreading rash.

Noticing my agitation, Angela says, "They weren't even here an hour, and it's still early. I doubt anybody will even hear about this. We're just lucky almost everyone at the paper is on vacation and they didn't send a photographer."

"I don't even think they cared about that. For most of them it was probably just a way to fend off summer boredom. For Bitsy, it was a personal vendetta."

"But like Dinky said, there's not much you can do about it."

"Maybe. But I'd like to know for sure." Picking up the phone again, I complete my call to Carolyn. "She's in court," her receptionist tells me. "Likely to be there all day. Do you want her voice mail?"

"No." I hang up, not entirely unhappy I can't reach her. I dial Alex's office instead. His machine picks up, and I leave a message for him to call.

The rest of the day is a blur. A few people—but not as many as I'd feared—phone to ask if Bitsy actually staged a demonstration in front of my store. Judging from business, it doesn't look like there's going to be a boycott. Orders have to be filled. A thousand small tasks have to be completed for the band concert at the end of next week, given that I might be gone a whole day for my trial. When Joey appears for her usual couple of hours, I don't even inquire about her hair. "You okay?" she asks repeatedly. I assure her that I'm fine. Thankfully, she hasn't heard about the demonstration. For once, I'm relieved when she finally goes to mail a package at the post office and then head home. By the time Angela leaves with our bank deposit and I close the shop, the day seems to have been about twenty hours long. The phone rings just as I'm walking out. I think about ignoring it, but am glad I answer when it turns out to be Alex.

"What's up? When Joey saw you today she thought you had the blues."

"Maybe not quite *the blues*, but bad enough." In a rush, I tell him about the demonstration, realizing as I talk that I've spent the past couple of hours letting it fester in my mind. "They had a permit, but you know better than I do if it was even legal."

"You say there was also a handout?"

I pick up Bitsy's flyer, its black letters screaming up at me from their garish yellow background, their very harshness a kind of accusation. "You want me to read it to you?"

"Why don't I drop by and read it myself? I'd like to take a look." Five minutes later, he's at the door.

I motion him to my desk, where he studies the flyer for what seems a long time.

"Isn't that libel? Or slander?" I'm ashamed not to know which is which. "After all, I haven't been convicted in court. At least not yet."

He takes off his glasses, wipes them with a tissue and puts them back on. "Slander has to do with the spoken word," he says patiently. "Libel is something that's written. Either way, this was uncalled-for, especially so close to the trail."

"I think Bitsy was just trying to take another jab at me," I say hotly, reminding him of my theory that she's still trying to get back at me for the essay contest. "She's competitive. More than anything else, she hates to lose, at tennis or anything else. She's not going to let up."

My own words chill me. "Nobody came from the paper, and they don't have any pictures, but if Bitsy or her friends mention it to the right people, they might end up doing a story." My mind does a mental flip back to the night of my arrest, when Alex heard about the photographer at my shop and told me in his iciest tone that I should have thought about

Joey before I threw the basket. My chest actually aches at the memory.

Lowering my voice, I say before I lose my nerve, "And if the paper does a story, Joey's name could still end up in it. I didn't mean it to happen this way. Please believe that. I'm so sorry, Alex."

A long sigh escapes from his chest. "The paper isn't going to go back on its policy of not printing minors' names," he says slowly. "I think Joey's safe. I'm not sure Bitsy and her lady friends will get any publicity from this, either. Putting on a dress-up parade to get attention is pretty transparent, and probably wouldn't make good press without a picture."

"So you don't think the paper will cover this even if Bitsy asks?"

"I think they'll see it for what it is, just a cheap gesture of...meanness." There's immense weariness in his voice. I suspect he's more worried about Joey than he wants to let on.

"Does Stephanie know about what's happened?" It's really none of my business, but I hope his ex-wife is sharing his parental concern. She's in England, after all, not on the moon. The only other family member close by is Jamene, who as his ex-mother-in-law doesn't quite count.

"Stephanie doesn't know unless Joey told her, and I don't think she did."

I nod, aware that Joey e-mails her mother regularly, but always puts a positive spin on events in Fern Hollow so Stephanie won't come rushing back to take her home before the summer is over. Jamene protects Stephanie for the same reason. Everyone is protecting everyone, except Alex. Alex is on his own.

He stands up, filling the small space between us. He lifts his hand as if to give me the flyer, then says, "How about if I hang on to this? Let me see what I can do."

I realize we haven't really discussed the issue of libel or slander, but I no longer care. I nod. He puts the flyer in his pocket. "LilyRose," he says softly, and what I hear, in tones so warm that I can feel the heat on my skin, is, *LilyRose, it's all right. LilyRose, you're going to be fine. LilyRose, don't fret.*

He says all this without uttering a word.

He moves toward me then. Although it's still a bright day outside, the room at the back of the store is windowless, lit only by a small lamp, which casts a cozy glow. For a moment I think Alex is going to embrace me. I feel myself already letting it happen, moving toward him with a joyful sureness I can't explain, anticipating the solidity of his chest, the brush of his whiskers, the strength of his arms.

Then I feel him change his mind. The joy vanishes; the world flattens to gray. His retreat is no more than millimeters, more a decision not to move forward than one to move back. Yet I feel it like pain, and see it as I always see pain: thin vertical lines in front of my eyes. He's not going to touch me. He isn't sure yet—neither am I—what will happen if the case ends up hurting Joey in some way. He doesn't know, in that event, if he'll even be on my side. If he has a choice, he'll choose his child, the bond that already holds him. Of course.

"I told your mother I'd be there for dinner," he says quickly.

"Better not keep her waiting." Both of us hear the catch in my voice, and both of us ignore it.

He walks me to my car and opens the door for me to get in. When he closes it, his hand rests on my window a few seconds longer than it has to before he pulls himself away.

I drive home, too tired even to eat. The day feels like it's lasted months. I fidget aimlessly most of the evening. It takes forever to fall asleep.

I don't expect to have the dream again. If anything, I ought to have a nightmare about Bitsy.

But no, there I am—floating with Alex beside me, not on water but in a velvet sky filled with undulating sheets of light, even more spectacular than before—huge, transparent flags of color. Pink and lavender and lime banners pass before us, a rainbow of pastels. Just looking at them is a kind of happiness.

We don't speak, but each of us understands that we want to touch the shimmering sheets of color. It doesn't happen. Every time we stretch our arms toward them, they shift and ripple and elude us.

Somehow, we touch each other instead. Not on purpose. Our fingers meet in the most casual way, and touch lightly across the distance. We float like that for a time. Not speaking, not embracing, just touching. Then we fall away from each other, apart, into the night. It is very hard to wake up.

Dressing for work, with my court date still a week away and the effect of Bitsy's mischief still unknown, fragments of my dream drift like puffs of cotton through my head. Its lack of conclusion disturbs me. Except for the basket incident, I wouldn't have known or cared about Alex except as Mama's tenant.

I wouldn't have had Joey as my apprentice. Deny it or not, now I care about both of them. For the first time since I threw that basket, I'm not afraid, only restless. I want to know what's going to happen, what's going to be possible—with Alex or without him.

For the first time, I feel ready to go on trial.

CHAPTER 14

Zee is alone in the house with Leona Richie when the thing happens that she knows will change her life. She tells herself later that she might have prevented it if she'd paid more attention, but she knows this isn't really true. Sometimes the future that has been inching up on you cannot be pushed back even another second.

It is the day of LilyRose's trial, so there is a lot on Zee's mind. She has just put on her third outfit of the morning, a lightweight gray pantsuit that looks dignified but not mournful, an appropriate mother-of-the-accused getup. The silky forest-green top she'd tried first was too dressy and not summery enough. Her second choice, a pink blouse, looked so frou-frou that she wondered what she'd been thinking. But the pale gray suit, lightened even more by her favorite clunky white earrings and necklace, will work whether the verdict is happy or sad.

According to LilyRose, her case is one of the first ones on the docket. Zee knows that doesn't mean a thing. Bettina Smith from church works as a court advocate for the domestic violence center and says that, depending what that gaggle of assistant DAs is up to, you could schedule a case for six in the morning and it might not be heard till noon. All the same, Zee knows LilyRose will have to be on time, and she wants to get there early to support her.

Fiddling with the clasp on her necklace, Zee wishes it didn't take so long for the coffee to brew. Nervous as she is, she's tired, too. She doesn't think she got a wink of sleep last night, fretting about LilyRose. It's true that this experience of being arrested and put on trial, for a perfectly understand-able and forgivable crime, has loosened LilyRose up some. Zee thinks she was right about that. But now she just wants it to be over.

Maybe she wouldn't be so antsy if she had let Kent come over, even just for dinner last night, but she wouldn't. She had the superstitious notion that it would be wrong to allow herself the pleasure of a man's company right before something so nonpleasurable as the trial. When she confessed this to him, he said don't be silly, all he wanted to do was help. But she insisted, and although he didn't press, she knew he wasn't happy about it. "I just wish you'd let me be more to you," he told her. This is not the first time he's said this.

Zee is not sure exactly what "more" means, and isn't sure she wants to. The whole idea that he'd like to explain "more" in detail makes her stubborn.

"You can't be more. You're already quite a lot," she says in the jokiest way she can, considering. "Besides, I'm almost sixty. Too old for you. You're practically a baby."

"Fifty-three is well beyond infancy. Well beyond adolescence, for that matter. If you were seventeen, you'd bore me to tears."

"What about thirty-five?"

"A trophy wife to bear my second family? No, thanks." Kent has been divorced for twenty years. His two children are grown. All the same, the term *trophy wife*, or even just *wife* scares Zee half to death.

"Okay. Forty-five. Fifty." Zee envisions Kent's ideal woman as someone with a petite build, not much taller than Kent, with far fewer wrinkles than Zee has and not a trace of gray in her hair. "I'm sure there are plenty of women out there who want you," she says.

"Oh, yes. All in hot pursuit of short, chubby corporate engineers. It's a growing problem in the industry. Corporate-engineer groupies."

This makes Zee smile, even though she would like to say sternly, *enough*. Zee doesn't like to admit that she's flattered by the way Kent is so open about wanting her. The concept of "more" scares her just enough to do things like forbidding him to come to dinner the night before LilyRose's trial, which wouldn't have hurt a thing.

In the end, it was just Zee and Leona Richie at the table last night. Alex went out right after he came home from work, saying he didn't know when he'd be back. Zee didn't invite Jamene like she might have otherwise, because she knew Jamene would start talking about the trial, and Leona would be all ears, and by the time the meal was over, Zee would be a nervous wreck.

She was a nervous wreck, anyway. Leona used to be good company, but lately she has a tendency to stare off into space and get quiet. Zee thinks this is because she is in pain, though Leona will never say so. Ever since her arthritis medicine was taken off the market because it could cause heart attacks, Leona has not been quite herself. It might have been better, after all, to listen to Kent and Jamene than to watch Leona staring out the window and not eating half of what was on her plate.

The coffeemaker finally stops dripping. Zee doesn't know why she made eight whole cups. There's nobody here to drink it. Usually Alex grabs a cup before he leaves and then pours another to take with him, but he went out early this morning and isn't likely to come back. She knows he's going to the trial, and Joey is, too. She bets he's taking Joey out to breakfast, and maybe explaining a few things, just in case Joey's name comes up during the testimony. For LilyRose's sake, Zee hopes this will not happen.

Opening the cabinet above the stove, Zee takes out the chipped Flower Power mug Cy got from the Philadelphia Flower Show. She pours her coffee into it, even though she has to be careful not to cut her lip on the jagged section where she has yet to glue the missing piece back into place. On an ordinary day, Jamene would drop in for coffee, too, and would be irritated that Zee had commandeered their mutual favorite cup. Zee would be pleased with herself for having done it.

But today she feels intensely irritated, having her cup and her kitchen all to herself. She doesn't feel *deserving*. Probably this is just nerves.

Looking up, she sees Leona Richie coming down the hall that leads from her bedroom to the kitchen. On any other day Zee would have heard Leona long before this, considering the noisy, shuffling, mincing steps she takes. Later, Zee chides herself for not being more observant. If she had been paying attention, would she have thought Leona's stride sounded different than usual? She'll never know.

Leona's fall isn't dramatic. One second she's inching her way toward the kitchen the way she always does. The next second she stops as if she's forgotten how to propel herself forward, and then drops—fairly gracefully—to the floor. She doesn't go down very fast, hit very hard or make any sound. She lies on the polished wood, her expression startled at first and then alarmed as she realizes she is unable to get up. The pain must hit her just then, too. She begins to moan.

Right away, Zee recalls the articles she's read in women's magazines, about how the fall doesn't always cause the fracture; sometimes the fracture causes the fall. The bones are so weak and brittle that one of them snaps, causing the victim to topple. Zee knows this is what must have happened. Leona didn't fall so much as she folded.

Afterward, Zee thinks she acted the way she did, so calmly, either because she wanted to get this over with and get down to the court—which isn't very charitable—or because she'd been expecting something like this all along. She knows better than to try to move Leona herself. She dials 9-1-1. Then she mentally goes through her list of who else to call. Leona's son, Nathan, needs to be notified, but since he's an hour's drive away, there's nothing he can do right this minute. First, she needs some moral support for herself.

She's not going to call Jamene, that's for sure. Jamene tends to get flustered rather than helpful when there's a crisis, and anyway, she's probably out with Joey and Alex on their way to court. Obviously she can't call LilyRose, since she's the defendant. She wouldn't want to call LilyRose right now even if she were available. LilyRose's "I-told-you-so's" about the dangers of a tenant being injured in Zee's house are already echoing in Zee's ears.

Briefly, she considers calling Alex, who is larger and stronger than anyone else on her list. She has his cell phone number somewhere. But if Alex is with Jamene and Joey, that would just bring the whole lot of them here, which is the last thing she needs. If the EMTs are going to lift Leona, she doesn't need Alex for his physical strength anyway.

That leaves just one person.

Kent.

Zee supposes she knew all the time he'd be the one she'd call.

Kent arrives just behind the ambulance. Together, they murmur comforting words to Leona as she is being loaded onto the gurney. "You're in good hands, Leona," Kent tells her. To which Zee adds, "You're going to be fine now, Leona. Everything is well under control. Don't you worry about a thing. I'll bring everything you need, and I'll call Nathan. We'll follow you to the hospital in the car."

An hour later, Kent and Zee are sitting in the orthopedics waiting room, where somehow the smell of antiseptic has seeped in, even though there are only ordinary chairs here, and a braided rug. Zee hasn't been in a hospital since Cy died. The odor of antiseptic brings all that back. She feels slightly dazed. Maybe in shock.

A doctor in a green scrub suit opens the door. His

posture and expression remind her so much of the doctor who told her Cy had broken his neck that he might be the same man. Zee knows he isn't. She is cold all over.

"Broken hip," she hears the doctor say. "Surgery as soon as her son arrives." She makes herself focus. Nathan is on his way. "Josh Morgan will operate. He's very good."

Very good? Josh is Paula Morgan's son. Zee was at his christening. When did he have time to grow up and become a surgeon? When did he have time to get "very good"? She feels like someone in a time warp, the antiseptic strong in her nostrils.

Kent squeezes her hand. "There's nothing more we can do here, Zee. We can go."

"Not yet." She sits as she sat then, not yet ready to take in what she's heard, aware as she was then that in some way the world has shifted and her life has changed forever.

"If we get to the courthouse soon, we might still hear the case," Kent says.

Zee nods at him. He seems to be speaking from a long way off. The world has shifted and Zee is back in the days of mourning, not just for Cy but the general dyingness of things—when even the death of some remote public figure or the sight of Cy's bronzed and decaying late-fall garden had her anointing every tissue in the house with tears. She'd hated herself for that, after so many years striving to be a person with a merry heart. Each day, she made herself dress as if she were going somewhere important, and faced the world from behind a smudge of gray eye shadow and the reddest lipstick she could find. From behind her painted smile, sometimes she almost forgot she was lying. Maybe, after a while, she *was* the lie.

She doesn't feel very good. Antiseptic has such a sharp, clear smell, you wouldn't think it could press down on you the way it does, like a too-tight body suit squeezing your life smaller and smaller, sending fog into your thoughts. She'd felt this way when Cy was here, and for a long time after—the pretense of cleanliness and normalcy in a place where nothing was really normal or clean.

Then Leona Richie had arrived on the scene and remedied all that. Zee had something to hold on to. A job. A boarding house. Things she needed to do. Useful, normal days.

That's over now.

"Come on, Zee," Kent says in a voice so commanding she can't ignore it. "I know you want to stay here, but they won't let you see Leona, anyway. You're her landlady. Not a relative. Not even really a friend."

That seems awfully harsh, but it makes Zee look at her watch. Court is already in session. They really do have to go.

Still, she doesn't move.

"Nathan will be here any minute," Kent says. When he grasps Zee's elbow and helps her up, she doesn't resist. If they stay much longer, the antiseptic will make her sick.

Getting off the elevator in the lobby, they spot Nathan coming in the front door, looking ashen and worried enough to need a stretcher of his own. Kent updates him on the situation and explains why he and Zee need to leave. Zee listens without adding anything. She is not quite herself.

"Hip surgery," she says dully when they walk outside. "She'll have to go to rehab. Maybe a nursing home."

"Yes," Kent agrees.

"She won't be able to come back to my house even if she recovers. Probably not ever."

"Probably not."

It's a beautiful day, hot but not the least bit humid, shot through with a clarity that begins to sweep the antiseptic out of Zee's head. They walk down the sidewalk, under the lush canopy of trees, listening to the small breath of summer making a swishing sound in the leaves. Then Zee says, suddenly and far too loudly, "So that's that. The end of my boarding house career."

Kent raises a puzzled eyebrow. "Why the end? Leona was just one tenant."

"Yes. The first and the last. I can't imagine taking in any others. LilyRose would drive me crazy about it. She'd be worried to death. To tell the truth, after this, I would, too." Zee feels perfectly lucid now. And not just lucid, but sharp. Bristly. Angry. "It's going to be lonely as hell."

Kent turns swiftly to regard her straight-on. This is probably the first time she's said the word *hell* in mixed company since high school, though she's thought it often enough. It's such a mild word, she can't imagine why she's been reluctant to say it out loud. But Kent actually registers shock. Zee looks back at him, defiant. Then she realizes he's reacting to her whole statement, not just the one word. Why would anyone be shocked because someone says the word *hell?* He seems to be lost in thought.

"It doesn't have to be that way," he says after a while.

"Be what way?"

"Lonely. You don't have to be lonely."

"No?" Zee suspects he's remembering the conversation they had the night after Bitsy's demonstration in front of LilyRose's store. The whole thing had upset her so much that she'd gone on a half-hour rant. "People like Bitsy wouldn't get so puffed up and self-important if they'd take a look at poor Leona!" she'd shouted then. "Poor Leona, all alone and hardly able to walk. If that little snot Bitsy knew how good she had it, there wouldn't be a demonstration or a trial, either one. And not just because of her money, either. In the end, all it comes down to is somebody to eat supper with and a sunny day and not too much pain." This was an oversimplification, but not by much.

Since there's no controlling the sunshine or someone else's pain, Zee knows what Kent is offering—someone to have dinner with, to be kind to, who will be kind in turn, and if they are very lucky, someone to touch.

A shiver runs all the way up and down her spine.

"There are a hundred ways not to be lonely," Kent says, as if he knows he's gone too far and is taking something back. "Maybe a thousand. I'll make you a list."

"Always the logical one."

"At the top of the list, of course, would be me."

"Of course."

"If that doesn't appeal to you, you could take in the homeless. Or children from third-world countries, awaiting medical treatment for highly contagious diseases."

"Thanks, but I'll pass."

"I'm just trying to offer you spiritual guidance," Kent tells her. Taking his hands off the wheel, he steers with his knees while he turns sideways to face her, folding his arms across his barrel of a chest and adopting a goofy, peaceful expression that makes him look exactly like a round, fair-haired Buddah. The worst part is, Zee finds this attractive.

"Drive with your *hands*," she orders, and Kent does.

She feels like she's been on a long journey, much farther than to the hospital and back. She checks her watch again. She hopes *to hell* she hasn't missed the trial. Some people have nothing. Zee has a daughter accused of a crime. What could she have been thinking, wanting to stay with Leona?

"There's also income tax," Kent says. "They always need volunteers to help the poor with their tax returns."

"You know how terrible I am in math."

"Or you could take in the spillover from the no-kill animal shelter."

"No animals," Zee says.

She feels a little better. She sees the kindness in the way he is giving her this choice.

CHAPTER 15

By the time I get to the courthouse for my trial, I'm hot and miserable and so nervous that my hands are sweating. Not clammy. Sweating. Tissues melt in my palms without solving the problem, and I can't rub my hands on my skirt to dry them because my outfit is such a light shade of pink.

Pink! Well, that's only my first mistake. It turns out you're told to arrive at nine so court can convene at nine-thirty, but everyone in Fern Hollow except me seems to know it never gets started until ten. You'd think my lawyer, Carolyn, would have mentioned this.

Mama said she'd get here early to give me moral support. Right now I'd settle for her cotton handkerchief to wipe my hands, but Mama is nowhere in sight.

If it weren't for the importance-of-well-groomed-nails lecture I often give Angela, I would start chewing off my newly applied polish right now.

Instead, I try to seem composed as I watch the other defendants and complainants and their families drift in. It's hard to tell who's on trial and who's not, because everyone sits on the same benches behind the banister. But one thing is for sure. My outfit is all wrong. Aside from being pink, it's an expensive business suit—straight skirt, fitted jacket, hot as the devil, that makes me look like an in-your-face-female applicant from *The Apprentice*. Almost everyone else, of either gender, is in dark, baggy slacks and a nondescript shirt. Clearly, the idea is to look as pathetic as possible.

What was I thinking?

Well, I know exactly. Last month Lavonne Patchett from Women in Business told everyone she'd been advised to wear a pink suit to the custody hearing for her children. It was supposed to make her seem well-adjusted and professional while at the same time feminine and motherly. It was supposed to render the judge sympathetic toward her. Apparently it did, because Lavonne got custody and her ex-husband got every other weekend. I see now that simple assault calls for a different strategy. It calls for black-and-white, not Technicolor, two sizes too big, not too new.

Well, too late now. Here I am. LilyRose Sheffield,
Pastel of the Year.

The courtroom gradually fills, mostly with people
I've never seen before, which is a little unnerving.
Even in a town as small as Fern Hollow, there are
certain residents more likely to have occasion to go
to trial. I never thought of myself as one of them.

Except for today, the only time I've been in
District Court was when I was on jury duty a year
ago. Along with thirty other prospective jurors, I'd
spent half the day in a holding room—a large, ugly
classroom with rows of hard chairs set on a not-too-
clean wooden floor. We were allowed to read but not
to make cell phone calls, and not to leave except for
lunch. Like students in detention, we even had to
raise our hands to go to the bathroom. Finally I was
lucky enough to be one of those called into the
courtoom to be considered for a jury.

It seems odd to me now, but back then I looked
at the courtroom after the seedy waiting area and
thought, *why, this is beautiful*—all rich wood against
pale walls, solemn and businesslike but not forbidding. I sat with the others on benches that looked
almost like church pews—not such a comforting
thought now, but very pleasant then—waiting to see

if we'd be needed for an auto theft case. The lawyers called us one by one, asked some questions, and either seated us in the jury box or let us go. I was disappointed when the entire jury was selected before they ever reached my name.

The difference between that day and this, aside from the fact that there's just a judge but no jury, was that then we were the only ones in the courtroom, and we weren't the ones on trial.

The more crowded the courtroom becomes, the more agitated I feel. Mama still isn't here, or Joey—for whom this is the event of the year—or even Angela, who will have to testify.

I don't see Bitsy, either. This worries me. After the fake civil-rights demonstration/boycott, she's been mighty quiet. As Alex predicted, there was no newspaper publicity. The message she was trying to send was a more-or-less private one to me, with a little help from her cohorts. But today is for the public, and I wonder what other kind of stunt she's likely to pull. She'll be wearing her shoulder sling again, for sure. She'll probably walk in at the last minute, dramatically supported on either side by her husband and friends. Not seeing her makes my mouth dry and my heart flutter. This is probably exactly what Bitsy is hoping.

Carolyn enters through the door for lawyers and court personnel. I'm relieved to see her, but instead of seeking me out right away, she stops to confer with a man holding the day's schedule. Carolyn is wearing a black suit even more corporate than my pink one, and carrying an enormous briefcase. In fact, all the female lawyers have large, new, expensive briefcases like Carolyn's, while their male counterparts seem to favor the sort of cheap fake-leather ones companies give away as a bonus for ordering office supplies. I wonder what this means.

A heightened sense of apprehension fills the courtroom as the clock inches toward ten, but the attorneys pay no attention. They're busy joking and slapping each other on the back, sending the message that relationships between legal colleagues are far more important than those with clients. To her credit, Carolyn doesn't slap anyone on the back. She spots the bench where I'm sitting and comes over.

"I checked the docket, and we're still one of the first half-dozen cases," she says. "Once this gets started, I think they'll zip right along."

"Angela isn't here yet," I say. Carolyn looks blank. "My assistant in the store," I remind her with a sinking heart. "I haven't seen Bitsy, either."

"Oh, they'll be here," Carolyn says blithely, and when one of the other lawyers beckons to her, she turns away. "See you in a bit," she says, and disappears.

Before I have time to be as upset as I think I'm going to be, or to wonder why Carolyn was recommended to defend me, Angela slides onto the bench beside me and squeezes my hand. "Don't worry, the perjurer is here," she whispers, proud of herself. "And the home team, too." She jerks her head toward the back of the room, where Alex, Jamene, Joey and Roberto are settling themselves into the last row. Joey catches my eye and waves.

"Only part of the home team," I say. "Not Mama." I'm halfway worried that something's happened to her, and halfway annoyed because I fear she's returned to the mindset she had when she didn't show up to get me at the jailhouse, and isn't going to show up here, either. I rub my sweaty palm on the wooden seat of the bench, smearing the wood with dampness.

The big clock on a far wall registers ten on the dot. The hum of nervous conversation grows edgy and a little off-key, sending a garish dance of orange and red splashes before my eyes. Then the bailiff strides to the middle of the room and in a perfect basso, barrels out, "All rise," and everyone goes quiet. Her Honor Patricia Morton sweeps into the room in her flowing black robe. She seats herself on the judge's bench, pounds her gavel and calls the court to order.

Let the games begin.

The first two cases zip along exactly as Carolyn predicted. The first one is dismissed after a few minutes of haggling among the lawyers; the second is continued to a later date. The third one is a shoplifting case involving a scraggly long-haired young man charged with stealing a can of paint from a paint store. The defendant is adamant that he thought the paint had been charged to the builder he worked for, and all he had to do was pick it up. He even signed a receipt for it, he says, but no one gave him a copy to take with him. The paint store has no record of any receipt.

The builder the defendant worked for claims he fired the boy a while ago, but is not sure whether that was before or after the shoplifting incident. As a businesswoman who writes paychecks, I can't see how the dates of employment can be in question. There is some discussion about whether the builder's account with the paint store was in good standing at the time of the crime.

One more case after this one, I think, and I'll be up. I check the room for signs of Mama. None. For signs of Bitsy. Ditto. I try to swallow, but my mouth is too dry.

The assistant district attorney, as if he's onstage in the center of a spotlight, rises importantly from his chair and announces he's calling the paint store manager to testify as a witness. "Jeremy Taylor," he booms.

I jolt upright, causing Angela to regard me with alarm. "Are you all right?" she whispers.

"Fine."

Then there he is, paint store manager *extraordinaire*, striding to the witness stand, his dimples every bit as deep as they were twelve years ago. He swears to tell the truth. Not only are my palms sweating, now my hands are shaking, too.

It's not that I haven't seen Jeremy plenty of times since our breakup. I have. Over the years I've run into him in the grocery store, in movie theaters, at the weddings of mutual friends. I've seen him with his first wife, Marti, who divorced him after two years, and more recently with his second wife,

Deborah. I've made note of the fact that the perpetual five o'clock shadow he was always so proud of has begun to be spiked with gray, although his hair remains uniformly dark. Is he dyeing his hair? Is he too dense to notice the color of his whiskers? Superior as these ruminations make me feel, I have reacted to each encounter with Jeremy exactly as I'm reacting today, with a bad case of the jitters. Each time I've asked myself, *why should this be?*

I was the one who ended our relationship, not Jeremy. I was the one who always knew his mustard-colored kisses weren't what I was looking for. I was the one whose life was better because of the career I pursued after I got rid of him. In spite of all that, in some way, I've always had the sense that there's something unfinished about all that, and it makes me feel…not scorned, not regretful, just uncertain. Shaky.

On the stand, he tells how the young defendant came into the store, selected one of the premixed shades of paint and walked out without paying. He did not come up to the cash register either to sign for the paint or pay for it with a credit card or cash. He simply left. Jeremy is very serious about this, all yes-sirs and no-sirs with the lawyer, as if he's giving critical evidence in an important murder trial. It seems pretty silly. Why not make the kid pay for the paint and be done with it?

Even with the knowledge of my upcoming case in a few minutes, I'm drawn into this. Jeremy is enjoying his time on the witness stand, you can see that. Well, of course he is. He's working at exactly the same paint store he worked at when I was going out with him, doing almost exactly the same job. He's probably bored to tears. This must be the most fun he's had in months. There's something almost gleeful about the way he savors each detail of his story. I wonder if the judge notices.

Judge Morton finds for the paint store. It's not exactly a victory. She fines the defendant the price of the paint plus twenty dollars in damages, an amount even this scruffy laborer should be able to afford. The sentence is clearly sending a signal not to bother the court with more cases like this. Both lawyers look chastised. Jeremy looks angry. He forces a polite smile as he shakes hands with his lawyer, but there's something about the tight set of his features that disturbs me. I'm still puzzling over this when my case is called.

Walking to the defendant's table, I quickly scan

the room again for Mama. By now I'm sure she's changed her mind and doesn't want to be involved in this any more than she did the day I went to the jailhouse. I'm sure the whole explanation of how she was proud of me for lashing out was just a ruse to get us to make up. I'm humiliated. I'm outraged. I'm hurt.

All these emotions race through me in the course of three or four steps.

Then I see her, at the very back. She doesn't nod or gesture in any way, but I know she knows I see her. It's as if we're connected. As if she's holding my sweaty hand.

I'm careful not to look around the room anymore. I don't want to catch sight of Alex. I can almost feel his eyes boring into me, daring me to be clever enough to carry this off without involving his child.

I take my place next to Carolyn. There's a quick explanation of what the case is about. Then there's a pause, which feels somehow unexpected. The two lawyers look at each other. The prosecutor seems bewildered. He stands up. "The plaintiff is not in the courtroom, Your Honor," he says.

Well, of course I know that. Bitsy is not here, but she will be. None of her friends are here yet, either.

Any second she'll march in with her entourage. Just as they did the day of the boycott, with their signs and costumes and camaraderie, they'll all arrive, *en masse*, with Bitsy herself in the lead. Her timing is always impeccable.

But the door at the back of the courtroom remains closed. My trial has come to a standstill.

"Counselor?" Judge Morton prods the prosecutor.

"If the plaintiff doesn't show up," Carolyn whispers to me, "the prosecutor can proceed anyway if he thinks it's serious enough. But ninety-nine percent of the time, he'll drop the case."

I hold my breath to stop the little flutter of jubilation that begins to build in my chest. Not yet, I think. Not yet.

"May we approach the bench?" the prosecutor asks. Judge Morton nods. He and Carolyn walk forward. The three of them confer.

An expression of resignation descends over the prosecutor's features. I take a deep breath. The case is dropped.

It all happens so quickly that it doesn't feel quite real.

People in a courtroom can't exactly burst into applause, but it's clear my cheering section is jubilant. After thanking Carolyn, I head for the hallway outside, where Alex and Joey and Jamene and Angela and Mama are waiting to congratulate me, as if I've won the lottery. "Now I can go to work," Alex says with a wink, and herds his family away. Watching his haste, the giddy elation I've begun to feel ebbs a bit.

"I'd better go, too, and relieve the know-nothing part-time help that's running your store until we get there," Angela says. "Of course, I'm a little disappointed I didn't get to give my testimony."

"You probably would have ended up in jail."

"We could have been cell mates," Angela says. "Listen, I can hold down the fort for a while. You go—have a milkshake to celebrate or something."

"Are you kidding? With ten thousand things to finish up before the band concert this weekend? I'll be there in fifteen minutes."

As soon as Angela's gone, Mama enfolds me in one of her big hugs. "Thank goodness," she murmurs. "I never saw you as a jailbird, but even so, I'm glad this is over." Releasing me, she furrows a brow and turns serious. "Why do you suppose Bitsy didn't show up?"

"Change of heart, I guess." We look at each other,

each of us aware that the other doesn't believe this. "That doesn't sound like her, does it?"

It doesn't. Bitsy is nothing if not persistent. It's a little scary.

"Well, who cares?" Mama says finally. "The important thing is, you're sprung. We're free."

I like the way she says *we*. Then I remember. "I didn't think you were coming."

"I almost didn't," she confesses. "Mrs. Richie is sick. I helped get her to the hospital, and I better go back now. Her son is there, but he looks sicker than she does."

"What's wrong with her?"

"We'll know more later." Mama shrugs but doesn't look at me. "Better run." She goes without even inviting me to dinner. She's in as much of a hurry as Alex was.

Four or five people come out of the courtroom in a silent cluster and walk slowly down the hall toward the elevator. Things must not have gone well for them. I don't notice Jeremy until he's right beside me. After his case was over, I thought he'd gone.

"Good job," he says with a smile that feels like a deliberate effort to show his dimples. "Tell me the truth. What did you do with Bitsy? Stow her somewhere?"

There's an edge to this, as if he really believes I might have. This is not a line of thought I want to pursue.

Seeing that I'm not going to answer, he changes tactics and studies my suit. "Good color for you," he says. Then, with a show of slyness, he adds, "Better than that orange you see when the Emergency Broadcasting System comes on, huh?"

What's *that* got to do with anything? "I haven't wrecked a car yet," I snip, and watch the half smile of satisfaction dimple his face when he sees me take the bait. It's the same expression he wore when he was accusing the young man of stealing paint, a twist of cruelty just beneath the handsome features.

A twist of cruelty. Yes.

I study him long enough to make him uncomfortable. "Why did you stay here, Jeremy?" I ask him. "Why didn't you go back to work right after your case was over?"

He's not expecting this. I watch him mentally change gears. "I thought maybe we could have coffee or something," he says lamely.

Right.

I know exactly why he stayed. He stayed because he thought it would be fun to watch me be convicted. He was hoping I wouldn't win. Like Bitsy, one of his great pleasures is watching someone else's humiliation.

Synesthesia? he'd sneered when I'd finally gotten up the courage to tell him. *Worse than crazy*, he'd said.

I guess this is why I've always felt we weren't quite finished—because until now I've been too insecure to acknowledge that the character flaw that ended our relationship wasn't synesthesia; it was cruelty. Not my flaw, but his. Even without admitting it to myself, I think I knew it wouldn't ever go away. Breaking up with him was probably more deliberate than I'd realized, and smarter.

As Mama has often pointed out, I am almost *too* good at protecting myself. Sometimes that works out for the best.

This is probably a fantasy, but I wonder now if the accused workman really *did* steal that paint. It would have been easy enough for a store manager to destroy a receipt showing the workman had signed for paint to be charged to his employer's account. How amusing for Jeremy to watch all that play out—except at the end, when the laborer's punishment didn't fit Jeremy's expectations, and his amusement turned to the anger I'd seen when he shook hands with his lawyer.

No wonder Jeremy has always given me the shakes.

The courtroom door opens again, and another group emerges, laughing, and heads to the elevator. "You sure you don't want that cup of coffee?" Jeremy asks.

"I'm sure."

"Let me run, then," he says, already striding away from me, toward the nearly full elevator that's about to close but doesn't until he steps in. He doesn't wave goodbye.

Then I'm standing there alone. Free to walk, not just out of this courthouse but away from Jeremy, too, now that the niggling term, *cruelty*, has been unleashed from the back of my mind. Like Angela said, I should really go have that milkshake—or something a whole lot stronger. I have no stomach for it. All summer worrying about this, and now my big victory, and here I am, loitering in the hallway outside the courtroom, solo, with a taste in my mouth as dark as burnt spinach. Alex is happy because Joey's name never came up. Ditto for Jamene. Angela is probably on the phone with her daughter, telling her what it's like to sit in court. Mama is not, after all, the mother of a convicted criminal—but not elated enough, either, to invite her daughter over for an evening meal.

Without anything—well, *anybody*—to hold on to, what do I have? I know: my freedom. I've always thought it was the most important thing. I still believe that. But now there's a barren quality to it, too—a spiraling hollowness, like falling through an empty sky.

CHAPTER 16

There's always more to do before a big event than you think there will be. I get back to the store right around lunchtime and don't leave again until nearly midnight. Dozens of tiny baskets still need to be assembled, and since I told Joey not to come today because of the trial, I have to do them myself. Angela is in charge of boxing and staging everything that's ready to go to the park in the rental truck we'll use on Saturday. Bonnie O'Dell will deliver some of the more delicate food items at the last minute. When we first decided how to do this, it sounded like a good plan.

Now it doesn't seem so workable. By the end of the day it seems we've barely made a dent in our tasks. Angela has fielded at least half a dozen phone calls about the trial, but I've had to take the rest of them myself. I don't mind, because they're from people I know well, and because they all have the general message of, "Oh, LilyRose, I'm so glad you won!"—for which I'm genuinely grateful. But in every case the congratulations are followed by, "Tell me all about it!"—and I spend, literally, hours doing that.

It's nearly closing time when Dorrie Sizemore calls, sounding even more excited than I was when they first dismissed my case. "And to think Bitsy didn't even show up! To think she went to visit her daughter at *camp!*"

"At camp? That doesn't make any sense." Bitsy is many things, most of them unflattering, but she has never been—at least until now—a no-show. All day I'd been half expecting her to turn up at the shop, having misread the time for the trial, and demand that I follow her back to court.

But to miss the trial because she decided to visit her daughter at camp? This sounds ludicrous. The basket I'd thrown at Bitsy was destined for Sally Ann at camp. Maybe the story had gotten somehow twisted?

"No, she went to the camp, I'm sure of it," Dorrie said. "I heard it straight from Ginny Evans." This is Bitsy's tennis partner and Dorrie's next-door neighbor. "Ginny said Bitsy left for camp early this morning."

"Was Sally Ann sick or something?"

"Not according to Ginny."

"Then why did she go?"

"Ginny said she didn't know. Just that Bitsy told her she was going to visit Sally Ann because she didn't have to go to court after all. The whole thing had been settled. I think she wanted Ginny to tell the country club ladies they didn't need to show up in court to support her—but that's just me reading into it. I'm not exactly in Ginny's inner circle." Dorrie seems as mystified by this news as I am, and a little miffed at Ginny for not giving her more details, but not inclined to doubt Bitsy's destination. As for me, I know that whatever Bitsy did today, whether she went to camp or not, Bitsy had a reason for, and it's probably a sinister one. But there's nothing like the raw panic of a looming deadline to blot out other emotions. The mountain of work still to be done, and the molehill that has actually been accomplished, make me forget Bitsy almost before I hang up the phone.

When I finally turn the Open sign to Closed at the end of the day, the situation hasn't improved. We need reinforcements, fast. After a few minutes of negotiation over the phone, Angela's daughter,

Mel, agrees to come over to help her mother fill boxes. Without any negotiation at all, Bonnie O'Dell says of course she'll help me finish the remaining baskets. Bonnie is turning out to be a treasure. Having retired—or so she thought—she grew bored after the first year, remodeled her kitchen to commercial standards, and began supplying the store again, with our most beautiful edibles. All week, Bonnie has been excited about the prospect of wowing the crowd at the park. She makes me feel almost lighthearted about our work.

Only once, when my fingers are busy but my mind has tuned out a discussion about whether to order pizza or Chinese for dinner, do my thoughts wander back to the courthouse. It's not the trial that comes back to me, but a vision of Alex's protective hand on Joey's shoulder after it was over. For the briefest second, it's like a physical jolt to realize that the joy in his eyes was for his daughter, not for me, and that my dreams of light and shivers of desire were based on the kind of adolescent fantasy I thought I'd left behind twenty years ago. I'm sure it was only my imagination, in the back room the other day, that Alex was about to embrace me. I'm genuinely ashamed. Glad as I am that Joey is safe from further ridicule, I'm humiliated, too. The thin vertical lines of pain that cross my line of vision remind me that even my friendship with Alex, having served its purpose, is probably over now, too.

Then Angela says, "My treat," as she picks up the phone to order food—pizza or Chinese, I've lost track—and my businesswoman self takes over and says, "Your treat? While you're working overtime for me? Absolutely not!"

We finally leave sometime after eleven. There's still plenty to do, but I sense that it will get done tomorrow even if we're exceptionally busy. For the first time in what seems an eternity, I fall in bed too exhausted to do anything but sleep, deeply and restfully, without a single troubling thought or—thankfully—any dreams about ribbons of light.

The next morning, Angela and I both seem to be regaining our sense of equilibrium. The preparations for the band concert are under control. Business is normal. Not wild, not slow, but pretty much what we expect this time of year. About an hour before lunch, when I spot Joey approaching from down the street, I feel that I finally have the energy to deal with her.

Little do I know.

She doesn't bounce into the shop as she usually does, or even stride, as she tends to do when Roberto is with her. She stomps. She frowns. She pouts.

"Well, this is all nice and cozy for *you*, isn't it?" she snips.

"Pardon?"

"You got off. You're free. Your business will probably take off like a shot now, and you're set for the rest of the year. You won't miss me not being around because you'll be able to hire all the help you want to. You're famous. Everybody in town will want to work here."

"Joey, what—?"

She interrupts before I can finish. "But *me*," she says. "*Me*." She strikes her chest with a dramatic thump. "All I get is to go back home. To go back to school. Great. Looking like this." She points to her head.

"Why don't we go to my office?" I guide her into the back before she can argue. "Okay. What's going on? What's this about, Joey?"

"It's about your life being picture-perfect, and my life being *shit*."

"Your life is *shit*?" No one should be surprised when a twelve-year-old uses this word nowadays, but somehow I am. "You care to elaborate on that?"

She glares at me in silence.

"This is about your hair, isn't it?"

"You're damn right it is."

"Sit down, Joey." I point to the chair beside my desk, but she keeps standing, and so do I, so close to each other in the tiny room that I can feel the angry heat radiating off her skin.

"Okay. Tell me about it," I say, crossing my arms over my chest in the hopes of showing I'm not about to take any nonsense. "Tell me why your hair is sending your life down the toilet."

"Because of Jennifer and Melissa, who are with me in just about every class," she says, equally no-nonsense.

"I take it Jennifer and Melissa are girls who don't approve of your hair?"

"Understatement of the year. Last spring they started an actual e-mail campaign about it. Jennifer would write, 'Your hair looks like a rat's nest—no offense.' Then Melissa would write, 'Your hair looks like shit today—just kidding.' Or something like that, every day."

"And what did you do?"

"What could I do? It probably looked just as bad as they said. You've seen my hair. It's thick. I was growing it for Locks of Love, that charity that uses human hair to make wigs for kids who've lost their own hair to a disease."

"I remember."

"It has to be ten inches long before you can cut it. At the end, my hair was completely out of control. There was nothing I could do with it. But everybody knew what I was doing. You'd think they'd have some compassion." Joey looks irate, not cowed in any way. "Finally, I did have it cut. The stylist said it was so thick, they'd probably be able to get two wigs out of it instead of the usual one." For a moment, her face registers a glow of pride.

"But you didn't shave it for Locks of Love, right? You just had it cut?"

"Right. Then the messages were, 'It's still a rat's nest. No, maybe a squirrel's nest. You are such a loser.'"

"And then?"

"Then I shaved it. I like to be proactive. I e-mailed my fan club back and said I *so* agreed with them about the squirrel's nest, so how did they like me now?"

"To get back at them?"

"Well, sort of."

"And did it work?"

This is when Joey's lower lip begins to tremble. "They said I looked like a cancer patient right after treatment." Her voice drops to a shaky whisper. "I guess I did."

I open my arms to her just as the tears begin, and she comes into them like the wounded child she is, and weeps the hot tears she's been holding back all summer. Soon I am weeping, too—not just for Joey, who lashed out against ridicule with a gesture that only invited more, but for my own final "How dare you?" in the flight of that basket, which might have caused her yet more pain, and maybe did. Clinging to each other, we weep for the stigma of baldness, the stigma of synesthesia, the sting of all the possible insults, whether they actually come our way or not…the misinterpretations, the ignorance, the simple pain of being *different*, the yearning to belong—we weep for all that until at last Joey's sorrow is only a damp circle on my permanent-press shirt and mine is only a hiccup in a dry throat spent of all emotion.

She leans against me for a long time, like a toddler on the edge of sleep. But I sense that she's fully alert; I am, too. "I'm sure you had some friends who didn't make fun of you," I say.

She sniffs, but doesn't speak.

"People surprise you sometimes," I say.

"I guess."

"I used to try to hide my synesthesia for the same reason you're embarrassed about being bald—because I thought people would make fun of it. Some of them did. But there was one friend who was better to me than I realized, who knew about the synesthesia but pretended she didn't because she thought it would make me self-conscious."

As I speak, I realize this is true. In the days after Dorrie put me in the drug program in high school, and in spite of Mama's admonition about keeping quiet, I'd tried to explain my condition to her. She'd smiled and nodded politely, but to me it seemed she thought I was making something up to wriggle out of a bad situation. It was clear that my story sounded so bizarre she couldn't get her mind around it and simply blanked out.

Now I'm not so sure. Now I think she knew and understood all the time, and pretended not to because she knew it would only make me uncomfortable.

"Sometimes," I tell Joey, "your friends are more loyal than you know."

She sniffs again, then says almost in a whisper, "There's Nicole, I guess," as if she's taken this so for granted that she's just remembered.

"See? She'll still be there when you go back to school, won't she?"

Against my chest, Joey nods.

"And here in town you have Roberto," I say. "He doesn't care if you're bald."

"Roberto is *ten*."

"Friendship isn't age-sensitive. A friend can be ten. A friend can be eighty."

"Or thirty-five?" Joey asks in a small voice.

"*Especially* thirty-five."

Very softly, Joey giggles.

All this time, I have been stroking her hair as she leans against me. It's as if my fingers realize first what my eyes have refused to see. I'm aware as I release her that anyone meeting Joey for the first time will think she has a rather strange, short haircut. It will never occur to them that she's bald. She's not. She hasn't been for quite a while. "Listen," I say. "I have an idea."

"What?" She wipes the back of her hand across a streaked and reddened face.

"How long until your school starts? Three weeks?"

"Four."

"Even better. You know what? I think your hair will be long enough by then to do something with." I run my hand along her temple, judging the length. "You might be able to get one of those punk hairstyles with the spikes sticking up."

"You think?"

"It could be interesting. It could be your fashion statement."

Tentatively, Joey pulls two pieces of hair up from the top her head, holding them in place like a pair of stubby devil's horns.

"That wasn't exactly what I had in mind," I say.

Joey isn't listening.

"And I could dye it," she says, already captured by this idea.

"Dye it?"

"You know, purple in one place—" she lets go of one of the horns "—pink in another."

I groan. "Just don't tell either one of your parents it was my idea."

"Don't worry." She catches sight of a pile of baskets in the corner, ready to be loaded into the truck. She frowns. "You look like you got a lot done without me."

"Only because I worked until midnight."

"So, you want me to help you out in the store today, or not?"

"Of course I want you to help. But you'll have to help Angela. I have to go out for a while. I have an errand to run."

"Where?"

"None of your business," I tease. "I'll tell you later."

In fact, I have no intention of telling her. My errand is to Alex, to tell him I've uncovered Joey's secret. To tattle on her. To ease his mind. It's just occurred to me that our connection isn't quite severed yet. After all, our friendship had a twofold purpose. Winning my trial was only half of it. The other half was finding out what was bothering Joey. If Alex isn't interested in me the way I imagined for a while, it's my own fault for letting my imagination get the best of me. He's worried. I can help him. If I'm any kind of friend, at least I owe him this.

CHAPTER 17

Although I've never been to Alex's office before, I know where it is. A kind of shaky joy fills me as I drive. Not only have I won my case, but I'm also the bearer of good news. Alex won't be able to help being glad to see me.

His office is on the second floor, up a long, steep flight of steps unbroken by a landing. After bounding up like a teenager, I'm rewarded with lungs screaming for air, a reminder that giving up the gym this summer in order to worry and fret was probably not a good idea. I stop to catch my breath and regain my dignity.

After one knock, Alex opens the door into a Spartan room furnished only with two computers, two wooden chairs and a fax machine. There's a single window looking down to the street, uncurtained and unshaded. Looking through the dust-filled block of light at the painfully austere surroundings where Alex spends his days, I become aware that Alex seems not to see the shabbiness. His voice wraps around me like a bright, weightless shawl. "Well! A guest. What brings you to my door in the middle of the day?"

"Lunch." I realize as I speak that I had this in mind all along. "After all the help you gave me with my trial, I feel like I ought at least to feed you before you hightail it out of town."

"I wasn't planning on hightailing immediately, but I'm always grateful for food. What did you have in mind? McDonald's? Wendy's?"

"What I had in mind was The Cloverleaf. Have you been there?"

"Not yet, but I've heard about it."

A few miles out of town, The Cloverleaf is Fern Hollow's premier eatery, set on sprawling grounds overlooking a magnificent pond. The building is a long, rambling structure with rooms leading into other rooms, each one windowed and airy, with French doors leading out to flagstone patios that dominate the hill above the water. Why I think I have time for a leisurely meal at a place like The Cloverleaf, I have no idea. But it's exactly where I want to take Alex. No place else seems remotely interesting or appropriate.

I let him drive. "Also, I have something to tell you," I say as soon as we get out of town and are speeding past lush green fields. "Joey finally confessed to me why she really shaved her head, and I can assure you, she's going to recover. In fact, I think she already has." I tell him what I learned, touched to see how he flinches when he hears about the cruel insults Joey endured from her classmates. I'm not sure I've ever seen a man so attuned to the raw, exposed nerve of a child's adolescence—except maybe Daddy, to whom I'm forever grateful for making me laugh at myself during those troubled years, at least once in a while. I still remember complaining about acne and expecting sympathy, only to watch him roll his eyes and say with complete irreverence, "Zits are God's punishment for being a teenager. They'll go away when you're twenty." As indeed they had.

This is not the first time it has crossed my mind that Alex is a good father the way my own father was. Yet it strikes me as odd that Alex's relationship with Joey reminds me of mine with Daddy, because the two men couldn't have been more different. Or at least different except in the caring—which I suppose is all that matters.

"I just want you to promise one thing," I tell Alex at last.

"What?"

"That if Joey dyes her hair purple, you won't think it's my fault."

"Promise," Alex says. We pull into The Cloverleaf's parking lot. "Don't get out of the car," he says. "I think this is one of those hoity-toity places where the man has to open the woman's door."

He takes my hand to help me out, a gesture that makes my blood feel so fizzy it might as well be ginger ale. I remind myself that today, this lunch, is probably the last chapter of our friendship. At best, we'll stay in touch by phone after Alex leaves Fern Hollow, or communicate by e-mail now and then. The thought is enough to un-carbonate a person's blood.

But it doesn't.

Our table is in the corner, with a view of the massive weeping willows at the edge of the pond, their delicate tendrils floating in the shallows. "I plan to break your budget," Alex says as he studies the menu.

"Please do."

"And after I order, I'll tell you how I got your case dismissed." He grins.

"*You?*"

A waiter appears then, a young man looking so uncomfortable in his black trousers and starched white shirt and sounding so anxious to tell us the daily specials that no matter how much I want to hear about my case and not the food, I feel it would be wrong to send him away. True to his word, Alex orders the lobster, the most expensive thing on the menu. Not to be outdone, I do the same. Several hours seem to pass while the waiter offers us our other choices—baked potato or fries, house salad or Caesar, a laundry list of dressings.

"*You* got my case dismissed?" I blurt the second the waiter turns his back.

"I did indeed." Alex takes a leisurely sip of his water. "I hit your friend Bitsy with a double-whammy."

"I'm assuming you don't mean 'hit' in the physical sense. And I'd appreciate your not calling her my friend."

"Suit yourself."

"So *tell* me," I urge.

"First I found out a little dirt about her on the Internet. It wasn't hard. And in case that didn't work, I also threatened to sue her for slander on

Joey's behalf. Actually, you gave me that idea your-self, that day you asked me the difference between slander and libel."

"You found out *dirt* about her?" I'm incredulous. Bitsy has always been one of those monsters lurking behind an incredibly clean shirt.

But Alex is serious. Between bites of salad and later the energetic work of cracking open and eating his lobster, he tells me what he discovered. Bitsy, whose maiden name was Winner, also had the last name Freeman for a time, some years before she married her present husband and became Bitsy Eversole.

"She changed her name?"

"She did. She was married for two years to a man named William Freeman."

Struggling to extract a sliver of lobster meat from its shell, I shake my head in denial. "No. Rick Eversole's her first husband. I remember the wed-ding. White dress, the whole shebang. She couldn't have been married before. This is a small town. Everyone would know."

"It was while she was away at college. He was a student, too. They eloped but kept it quiet, maybe so their respective parents would keep paying their tuition. A week before they graduated, he got arrested and ended up in jail."

"Jail! For what?"

"For stealing a car. That was the end of the romance. Bitsy's parents stepped in and had the marriage annulled. The whole thing was very hush-hush. But there are certain records that aren't too hard to dig up, if you have a mind to."

I stare at him, having trouble taking this in.

"I don't know who else knows about it. Bitsy's husband, Rick, possibly, but probably not his family. The upstanding Eversoles. I figured Bitsy wouldn't be anxious for them to find out now, after hiding it from them all this time."

I sit there, flabbergasted. "Were you really going to tell?" I finally ask.

"Probably not. I wasn't going to sue her for slander, either. Once you start a suit like that, it's all on the public record. Joey would have been big news, which is the last thing I wanted. But Bitsy didn't know that. So I convinced her that instead of going to court, it might be a good time to visit her daughter at camp."

"Then it was true!" I laugh. A huge weight seems to have lifted from me. I forget the work awaiting me back at the shop. "Dorrie's neighbor told her Bitsy went to camp, but I wasn't sure I believed it."

"See? I saved your bacon. I'm a genius."

"You *are* a genius. But I think it's Joey's bacon you wanted to save."

Lobster can be a messy meal to eat, even after lots of experience. Both of us have piles of shells on our plates and grease on our mouths from the butter we've been dipping white lobster flesh into, so when Alex's expression turns serious and he says softly, "Not just Joey's bacon. Yours, too," at first I don't take this in fully because I'm too busy studying the slick spot on his chin and thinking that, on Alex, it doesn't look half-bad.

"What?" I say.

He puts down his little lobster fork and wipes his chin with his napkin. "You were always a big part of this, LilyRose," he says. "I thought you knew that."

I give myself a moment to absorb this. "You've been very kind," I say.

"Not kind. I did it because I care for you." He bunches up his napkin, then remembers to put it back into his lap. "I did it for you personally, not just for Joey. Do you understand?"

I'm not sure I do, but I put down my own fork and let the approval in Alex's eyes wash over me until the fizz in my veins makes my fingers tingle. I don't exactly ignore the telltale tug low in my belly, but for once I don't try to censor it, either. "I hope I understand, Alex," I say.

"I didn't want to say anything…well, *do* anything…until the trial was over. I was afraid if I did, you'd feel pressured into—well, into reciprocating whether you really wanted to or not. I didn't want us—didn't want whatever there might be between us—to be clouded by that."

"You didn't?" I say stupidly.

"No. I know I made you feel guilty about getting Joey involved. I knew it wasn't your fault. I wanted to apologize, but I didn't know how you'd feel about me, depending on what happened at the trial. I thought it was wiser to wait."

"You were going to apologize?" I sound like a parrot miming its owner. Alex doesn't seem to care.

"I *am* apologizing," he whispers, and reaches across the table to take my hand. Despite our efforts with our thick cloth napkins, both of our hands have remained a little slick. The grease seems to enhance the speed at which the tingling in my fingers is transferred to his—or maybe vice versa. Both of our hands are trembling.

"You waited," I say.

"Yes."

In my experience, men do not wait. This is the moment when it occurs to me that there is a difference—sometimes a chasm—between lust and love.

I censor the word *love*.

I pay the bill quickly. My belly isn't nearly as full of shellfish as it is with an emotion I'm afraid to name, and my throat feels so thick that I'm afraid if I speak, I will sound like my voice has changed. I consider the option of not going back to work. Of inviting Alex to my house, instead. Of letting Angela make sure the barbecue preparations get finished, which I'm sure she can do.

Alex's hand is at my waist as we get up to leave, and for once—for that moment—my life feels exactly right.

Then I see Mama. Silhouetted against the window in the next room, she's sitting at a table across from Kent Oliver, her ex-tenant. They're leaning toward each other across a basket of the restaurant's signature cloverleaf rolls, which for all their appeal seem to be untouched. Kent and Mama are talking, nodding their heads, gesturing, not in a landlady-tenant way but in a manner that suggests urgency, intimacy, shared personal secrets. I am so stunned that I stop short and stare. As if she feels the intensity of my gaze, Mama looks up. She sits up straight. She puts on an embarrassed smile. Then she notices Alex with his hand at my waist, and the guilty look fades and she raises her eyebrows.

There's nothing to do but head in her direction to say hello. "Mama!" I say in a bright voice that seems to belong to someone else.

"LilyRose!" As if we haven't seen each other for years. "What are you doing here?"

"I took Alex to lunch to thank him for his help with my trial," I offer by way of explanation. "I didn't expect to see *you* here."

Mama opens her mouth as if to reply, but nothing comes out. It's Kent who answers. "Your mother can't go out to dinner because of having to cook for tenants, so I convinced her to come to lunch," he says.

I don't believe this. I don't think Kent does, either. After all, he and Mama have dinner together every night. He's one of the people responsible for her having to do all that cooking.

"My car wouldn't start this morning," Mama adds

in a whisper that makes her sound like someone with laryngitis. She lifts her glass, takes a long swallow of water, then says more strongly, "Kent took me over to the farmer's market so I wouldn't miss it. He has a few vacation days this week."

This is explanation number two, so I don't believe this one, either.

Mama and Kent exchange a loaded glance. I see that their meeting is no more about cooking for tenants or visiting the farmer's market than my own meeting with Alex is about Joey.

"You ready for the band concert?" Mama asks. She is practicing Jamene's strategy of sticking to small talk.

"Almost ready. But I won't be if I don't get back to the store." I take Alex's arm and let him usher me toward the door.

"It's not just Kent eating dinner there because he doesn't like to cook," I snip the instant we're outside. "It's this whole other—this whole other *dynamic*. I feel like a complete fool. Why didn't you tell me?"

"Me?"

"You eat there, too, don't you?"

"Yes, and I can report that never once did I see them making eyes at each other over collards and cornbread." Alex opens the car door for me with annoying calm.

"I suppose they go to movies as well as the farmer's market and every other place in town," I lament as we drive off. "I'm probably the only one who doesn't know."

"No doubt." Alex's mildness mocks me.

"Well, she should have told me. It's not as if they're—" I want to say *lovers* but the word won't come out.

"They're not what?" He knows perfectly well what I mean. "Well, what if they are?" A slight smile plays at the edge of his mouth. It's the most irritating expression I've ever seen.

Any jabs and stabs of desire I'd felt back at our table, any notions about tingling hands and a soda-pop circulatory system and the aphrodisiac effects of seafood have now been replaced by something more akin to indigestion.

My mind is a jumble. Alex and I will not be going to my house as I'd imagined, not making that leap of faith I'd thought we were both ready for, that might have taken us—where? To a place where we might ride helpless on the tide of our own pleasure? What a cliché.

"I have to get back to work," I tell him. "The band concert's tomorrow."

Actually, I'm not thinking about the band concert at all. I'm thinking that I have to settle this with Mama before I do another thing. Until I talk to Mama, I'll barely be able to breathe.

All the same, I'm disappointed that Alex doesn't argue with me. We ride the rest of the way into town in silence. After parking his car behind his building he walks me to mine and thanks me politely for lunch. Then he disappears into the door that will take him to his monk's cell of an office. And that's that. Romance thwarted. Or maybe just sex.

I check in with Angela and return a few phone calls to give Mama time to get home. She must be expecting me when I get there, because hers is the only car in the driveway. I remember taking her to have it serviced only a few weeks ago. I'd be willing to bet Bountiful Baskets that it's still starting up like a charm.

I mean to tackle the issues between us in a mature and measured way, but the moment I shut the door behind me, I blurt, "You! And Kent Oliver! Why didn't you tell me? Is he your friend? Your lover? What?" I drop my purse on the table and begin to pace the kitchen floor. Mama stands by the stove, so motionless that I begin to feel like some out-of-control windup toy. I make myself stop.

"Not that I need your permission," Mama says finally, "but Kent is...my gentleman friend. It's just like he told you—he's someone to have lunch with, since I have to be at the house for dinner. He's someone to talk to."

"He's more than that."

"Well, recently—yes."

I want to add, *not to mention that he was a tenant*, but after my lunch with Alex, that's pretty much a moot point.

"He's important to me, LilyRose," she says. "Until lately I didn't know *how* important, so there was really nothing to tell."

"Except that you were *seeing* him."

"I see a lot of people. I didn't think it was anybody's business but my own."

Nobody's business but her own? I've never heard her say a thing like that. She points to a chair. I shake my head and cross my arms defiantly.

"First and foremost," she says, "Kent is a good friend but not the love of my life. Your daddy was that. I want you to understand that even if Kent becomes the love of my *current* life, there would be no disrespect in that to your daddy. Do you understand that?"

Not at all.

"I've thought about this a lot. I loved your father. I've tried to honor his memory the best I know how. Taking care of this house, getting you to tend his garden— But sometimes I go out into that yard and I swear, LilyRose, it's like he's standing there, looking disgusted, saying, 'You've still got a few good years left, Miss Zee. Don't hold on so tight. Better keep on blooming.' I think that's what he would have wanted."

Mama is not a *Twilight Zone* kind of person, so I think she believes this. It seems too mean to argue with her.

"Sit down, LilyRose," Mama tells me. "I'm going to tell you everything that's happened."

Over the next half hour, she does. She tells me about Leona Richie's hip operation. She tells me that once Alex leaves, she'll shut down her boarding house entirely. She tells me she might travel to Europe with Kent, come fall. She isn't sure. She doesn't ask for advice. She doesn't apologize. She doesn't back down.

I see that she doesn't belong to me anymore the

way she once did—or to Kent, either, for that matter (which is kind of a relief), but only to herself. I think I've been waiting for this for a long time.

"I know you're thinking it would have been easier for you if I'd kept you posted all along. But until the last couple of days there was nothing to keep you posted *about*. Anyway, you were always so opposed to tenants."

"I was afraid for you, Mama. That's all."

"I know, and you were right. Tenants *are* dangerous."

My heart gives a little flutter. "What are you saying, Mama?"

"It seems to me that you were having lunch with your own secret gentleman friend today," she says with a wry smile. "And that he was a tenant, too."

"There's nothing to it," I tell her.

"Maybe not." She doesn't sugarcoat this at all.

Driving back to the store, I wish I hadn't overreacted to the sight of Mama at the restaurant and pushed Alex away. But maybe it's just as well. In my dream, Alex and I could never touch those ribbons of light. Maybe my life will always be this way—disappearing banners of light, music rising to a crescendo but never getting there, the summery ripeness of raspberry sherbet hovering in the stratosphere while earthy lemon tartness is the best I can get, or mustardy, Jeremy-Taylor-style fluff that tasted rotten even when I thought I was in love.

I had the right idea twelve years ago when I decided to concentrate on my career. If I'm not anticipating the barbecue at the moment, if I'm feeling nostalgic for the medley of emotions I experienced back at the restaurant, what difference does it make? The magic of the afternoon is gone. Time to pour my energy into the task at hand. I remind myself it's a job I'm lucky to have. This is what I'm about, isn't it? LilyRose Sheffield, Merchant of the Year.

CHAPTER 18

Early on the day of the barbecue, Zee stands on the flagstone path in her backyard, aiming the garden hose toward the bed of climbing roses beside her kitchen. She's not doing this because the plants need water—for all she knows, she's drowning them. She's doing it because it's such a pleasant task. The arc of water gurgles through the air, then disappears into the soft mulch beside the roses. No one else is up yet, and Zee is filled with the lonesome, early-morning happiness of high summer, which seems all the sweeter today because she knows it won't last. Already she can feel the season beginning to change. The days are getting shorter, and although it's still hot, the afternoon sunlight is more golden, no longer the white blaze it was a few weeks ago. When Zee turns off the water, her bare feet on the walkway feel cool.

Rolling up the hose as she studies the back of her

house, Zee finds that the crumbling stone patio and dripping air conditioner jutting out of the kitchen window make her feel almost motherly toward the place. Even with Alex still in residence, the house feels more *hers* than it has for quite a while. She supposes that's because of the call she got late yesterday about a prospective tenant, and the way she listened to herself say (as she had just said to LilyRose not an hour before) that she was closing up shop.

"He's one of our top executives," the woman from corporate headquarters persisted. "It's only for a couple of weeks."

"No. I've decided." But Zee had felt a little pang of indecision tugging at the back of her throat.

And then! Not ten minutes later the nervy would-be tenant appeared at her doorway in person, a big, white-haired, gray-suited fellow, very elegant and sure of himself.

"I know you said you're not taking anyone in," he said, indicating the house with a hand as large and hairy as a gorilla's, if gorillas wore expensive pinkie rings and filed their nails. "But I'm hoping I can convince you to change your mind. It's only for a short time. Please. I hate hotels. I'm sure we can work out some financial arrangement. Can I come in?"

Zee didn't like him mentioning money so quickly, as if she were a pauper who'd change her plans for cash, but she thought it only polite to give him a cup of coffee, now that he had asked. "Lovely home," he said, and began to quiz her as if they'd reached some agreement. She did not offer to show him a room.

"I understand you serve dinner," he said. "I don't eat much meat." He patted the area above his heart.

"Well." Zee had never believed lean beef clogged arteries. She believed unhappiness did. "I'd like to help you, but I'll be traveling," she told him. This was not necessarily true. Kent wanted Zee with him on his business trip to London, but she was afraid of flying and even more afraid of living in a hotel with him *as his mistress*, though the idea did make her feel daring. She cleared the executive's coffee cup from the table without asking if he wanted more, and showed him the way out.

She was not usually so mean-spirited toward people who came to her house. It rather surprised her. Watching him get into his car, she knew with complete certainty that the decisions she'd made these last few days had been for the best. She simply did not want to cook or share her home any longer with people she didn't care about. She didn't want to be responsible for another Leona Richie, and certainly not for some aging corporate bigwig with heart problems. Family and friends, yes. But strangers? She'd been over this in her head a hundred times. But this was her first chance to test the point in practice. She was glad to be able to say no.

Now, hearing the side door to the house quietly open and close just outside the gate, Zee turns with a slow smile, sure it must be Kent, whom she left upstairs in her bed, sleeping. He must have gotten up and remembered something he needed from his car.

But when she peers beyond the fence toward the grassy area everyone uses for parking, she sees it's not Kent, it's Alex. His hair is still wet from his shower, and his khaki shorts and short-sleeved shirt look newly pressed. If she were Jamene she'd wonder why he's up practically at the crack of dawn on a Saturday, earlier than he usually gets up even on the days he goes to work. In particular, Jamene would wonder why her ex-son-in-law is looking so spiffy. But although these questions run through Zee's mind, she doesn't really care. She's just glad he's leaving, and that for a little while, she and Kent will have the house to themselves.

Heading inside, Zee automatically takes a deep breath as she climbs the back steps, where in early summer she'd get a heady whiff of the roses. But at this time of year there's no scent. The leaves of the bushes are still glossy and healthy looking as a result of LilyRose's spraying for black spot, but they won't bloom or release their heavy fragrance again until next spring. Zee thinks that's just as well. From now on, the smell of Cy's roses will always be tied up in her mind with that first night Kent took her up to her room. She will always feel a little guilty about that.

On the other hand, she doesn't feel guilty that he's up in her bed right now, where she's about to join him. Nor does she feel guilty that, later, she will go with Kent to the barbecue in the park. This will be the first time she's ever gone with any man but Cy, whom she met there more years ago than she'd like to remember. She ought to be bothered, but she's not. She thinks Cy would say, "Good for you, Miss Zee. Enjoy that good barbecue sauce while you can." She does not think he would say a single thing about her companion.

Zee doesn't think he would criticize the other thing, either—that Kent has suggested, in the most tentative way, that sooner or later Zee might want to sell her house and buy a new one with him—a house that will not be his or hers, but theirs. Possessive as she is of this place, especially now that she's giving up being a landlady, she knows Kent has a point. If he becomes a permanent fixture in her life, this won't be a place of business anymore, just the home she lived in for so many years with Cy.

Then it strikes her that if she and Kent ever have a house of their own, the yard won't be beautiful like this one, just a jumble of sticks and weeds. Kent doesn't have any more of a green thumb than Zee does. She's not sure if this is an argument against living with the man or just another instance of her mind going all over the place, as it has so often the past week or so.

What will happen to her? Will she get up the nerve to go to London? Will she stay with Kent? Sell her house? Start all over? Zee has no idea. She smiles. All this uncertainty! It makes her feel young.

Young! By seven in the morning I've been up for hours and feel about ninety years old. Crick in my back. Eyelids heavy from lack of sleep. Pulse racing from too much caffeine. And that smirk on Bonnie O'Dell's face! "C'mon, LilyRose, hand me those baskets. You can do it, girl. You're *young*."

Young. I don't even *remember* young.

Deciding to load the truck and set up the booth this morning rather than last night was a big mistake—but it was *my* mistake and I ought to be making the best of it. So why am I griping? Unlike me, Bonnie didn't get any sleep at all. She was up all night baking. Yet here she is, cheerful as sunshine. Get a grip, LilyRose.

I force myself through the motions of supervising the work, all the while re-running the memory of yesterday evening, when I got out of my car in front of my house hoping for a few hours of reprieve. The last thing I expected was to find Bitsy Eversole perched on my front steps. There she sat, her tanned legs stretching out from beneath her white tennis skort, half-empty bottle of spring water in her hand, watching me come up the walk as if she owned the place. It wasn't until I got closer that I saw how weary she looked, as if she'd been sitting there a long time. I hoped she had.

"Well," I said, at a loss for a better greeting. I

didn't recover myself until she began to stand up. Then I cut off any expectation she might have of being invited into the house by quickly gesturing for her to stay put and plopping myself down beside her. "What's on your mind, Bitsy?"

Rather than answer right away, she looked beyond me, scanning the trees on the other side of the street as if contemplating some deep truth I was too stupid to grasp. "I think we need to call a truce," she said.

"Oh?" A truce? Bitsy? Besides, I thought I'd already won the war. But this assumed she didn't have something else up her sleeve, which was always dangerous when dealing with Bitsy. "What are you suggesting?" I asked.

"I know I insulted your little friend," she said, unable to keep a trace of malice out of her voice. "But then you threw a basket at me. So I picketed your store. When you went to court, the case against you was dropped." She set her water bottle on the step and ticked off each point by clicking a baby-pink nail on the concrete. "I think we're even?"

I waited long enough before answering to watch her squirm uneasily. Then I said, as coolly as I could, "I thought you wanted to get even by sending me to jail. I thought you wanted to make me a jailbird to prove it didn't matter that you'd married one."

Bingo! For a nanosecond, she looked as if she'd had the wind knocked out of her. A flicker of alarm flared in her eyes, and her expression grew as raw and unguarded as I'd ever seen it. It was gone in a heartbeat, but it was enough to let me know why she'd come here. She knew Alex had uncovered her well-protected secret. But she wasn't sure if I was in on it, too. If he hadn't told me, she could continue to wage war in a small way. If I knew...that was another story.

As quickly as she'd revealed herself, Bitsy lowered her usual veil of disdainful calm. "I have a child," she said. "I'd just as soon she never found out about—" she managed a wry smile "—about the jailbird," she finished.

I wasn't sure if I felt more sympathy or more disgust. You'd think someone with such deep feelings for her daughter wouldn't insult someone else's child for being bald. But Bitsy is Bitsy.

"I wasn't planning to spread the word," I said, and then decided Bitsy wouldn't take me seriously unless I threw in at least the hint of a threat. "Not now, anyway."

"Good," she said, ending the interview. Never one to engage in prolonged chitchat with the riffraff, she stood up and smoothed her skort. She didn't thank me. I didn't expect it. She didn't bend to retrieve her water bottle. She didn't look back.

For all her posturing, the war was over. There was no glory in her stiff-backed retreat. Both of us knew the confrontation had ended for good.

Did I feel victorious? Maybe, just a little. Mostly, I was weary. Inside my house, I flopped down on the couch and immediately began thinking of details I needed to tend to in order to get today's booth running smoothly. I made furious notes all evening. Throughout the night, I kept jerking awake and turning on my light to write down something else. It was almost a relief when, at a truly alarming hour, the alarm clock finally rang.

Now, with a clear dawn breaking over the late-summer sky and my third cup of coffee getting cold as I orchestrate the loading of the truck, my nerves are thoroughly jangled. When Bonnie tells me I should be moving faster because I'm *young*, some-how I seem to have forgotten the meaning of the word. I have to remind myself again that I might not have slept well, but Bonnie has twenty years on me and didn't get any sleep at all because of the baking. Yet here she is, cheerful as sunshine. *Focus*, Lily-Rose. You've been waiting for this day all summer.

After what seems like an eon, we're finally ready to drive our first load of supplies to the park. We'll unpack, make another run back here to the shop because I was too cheap to rent a bigger vehicle, and then get the booth ready for customers before the gates opens for the barbecue. Is this even remotely possible? At the rate Angela's daughter, Mel, is filling boxes with cookies decorated to look like the drums the Fern Hollow High marching band is famous for, we'll be ready about the time the park closes at midnight.

Then, wonder of wonders, guess who pulls up beside the truck in the parking lot? Alex. "I told you I'd help you set up," he says, all business. "What do you want me to do?" He doesn't sound like he's forgiven me for cutting off our brief flirtation in order to confront Mama. He just sounds dutiful, a man making good on an offer of help he made in the days when we were phone buddies.

Despite his cool demeanor, Alex looks terrific, which seems like a rebuke. His clothes are off-the-rack tidy. Mine are wrinkled and smudged. He smells like soap. I'm pretty sure the rest of us smell like sweat.

So be it. This is no time for thoughtful ruminations.

"How about driving the truck to the park and helping us unload?" I ask. Beneath his short sleeves, Alex's male biceps look remarkably appealing, able to lift whole trays of fudge in a single swoop. "I need Angela and Mel back here at the store to finish packing, but I want to park my own car near the booth in case we have any emergency errands to run later."

"Done," Alex says, and plucks the keys to the truck out of my hand.

For the next few hours, he works as if he has as much invested in this as I do. Without being asked, he helps me assemble the lightweight racks brought from the store to hold the little gift baskets I've made. When Joey arrives with Roberto, he backs up my suggestion that the two of them pin festive red skirts to the display tables. These will hide the coolers underneath, filled with the beautiful but impractical sweets Bonnie O'Dell insisted on bringing—delicate chocolates, cherry tarts, even a few tiny cheesecakes she's promised she won't charge for if they don't sell. On a more sensible note, Bonnie arranges her ever-reliable, prepriced cookies in a display that makes them look even more mouth-watering than usual. Impossible as it seemed, the booth begins to take shape. When Alex leaves to make a final run to the store, I realize that all morning I've been aware of his nearness in a way that would disturb me if I had more time to think about it. Then he's back, with Angela and Mel and the last of the supplies. We unload the truck with a synchronicity we might have been developing for years. I pretend not to notice. Finally we're ready. When I turn around to thank him, Alex is gone.

Then the park opens, and from that moment on, we're busy. Angela takes charge of the cash box. Bonnie conducts herself like saleswoman of the year. Joey and Mel replenish the rapidly emptying displays. A few hours pass before I even have time to notice the smell of pork and chicken barbecue wafting up from the cook pit down the hill. I pause briefly to note the slight rumbling in my stomach, and pop one of Bonnie's decadent chocolates into my mouth to stave it off. Then I return to the tasks at hand. The desserts, the souvenirs…everything is selling. It's all we can do to keep up with business.

Throughout the morning and into early afternoon, my only sense of passing time comes from the strains of music drifting from the bandstand. Before the day is over, practically every band of every description from the tri-state area will perform. Scheduling them is always a political nightmare. The less skilled bands are relegated to the early morning, before the park gets too crowded and anyone can be too embarrassed by the sound. After that, the quality of the music improves exponentially as the audience builds, except when some amateur band with political pull has managed to finagle a desirable slot. By evening the program will feature one fine regional band after another, playing everything from bluegrass to beach music to pop. As the hours pass, the shapes in front of my eyes go from annoying (jagged black lightning bolts) to not-so-annoying (bouncing pear-shaped balls) to relatively pleasant. But not until Joey taps me on the shoulder between customers and asks if it's okay to take a break do I actually look at my watch. Nearly two-thirty. "Oh, honey, of course you can take a break! I didn't mean to keep you here so long."

"I don't mind helping," she says. "It's just that—" she gestures vaguely to the side of the booth "—someone's waiting for me."

Looking over, I expect to see Roberto, but it's a girl, probably her first female friend of the summer. Or—no, it's two girls, their ponytails bouncing behind them as they wave and try to get Joey's attention.

"Well, go on before you starve to death!" I tell her. "Have fun!" And she's off in a flash.

This reminds me to give Angela and Bonnie a break, too, and to send Mel home, since she agreed to work only half a day and has been here far longer. The day is hot but not humid, so at least no one seems about to faint from the heat. During the after-lunch lull, I'm alone in the booth for the first time when Daddy's old friend Crusty Caster wanders over, buys one of Bonnie's tiny, all-too-meltable cheesecakes, and nibbles on it while he checks out the rest of the display. Crusty, who would take offense if anyone ever addressed him as Mr. Caster, has been on the town council ever since I can remember. I wonder whether he's the one who kept them from firing me after my arrest and Bitsy's big fuss.

"You don't have to be nice and buy anything else, Crusty," I tell him. "For me, it's enough just to be here today. I heard the town council was thinking of getting rid of me after—well, after the incident with Bitsy."

"You heard that, did you?" Crusty sinks his teeth into another bite of cheesecake and regards me with open amusement.

"I didn't mean to hurt her," I say automatically.

He raises an eyebrow—*gotcha*. "No?"

"Okay. Maybe I did," I admit. "She insulted a friend of mine."

"So I heard."

"But is it true that the council nearly canceled my contract? I kept hearing it, but then nothing happened. Was I really about to be fired?"

Crusty lets me wait a long moment, during which the mingled odors of barbecue and cheesecake hang in the air. Then he winks and says, "Not even close. Even with Bitsy having her hissy fit, it never entered anyone's mind."

I'm not sure if this is true, but I'm glad to hear it.

By the time Angela and Bonnie return, we're busy again. Late-afternoon snacks go quicky, and young parents grab up small souvenirs to please their tired, fussy children while also signaling the end of the day. When Mama and Kent finally wander over, wanting one of the miniature baskets

I'd put together, every one of them has already been sold.

"Why, that's wonderful, LilyRose," Mama says. "By the time this is all over tonight, you won't have a single thing to take back to the store."

That's an exaggeration, but I don't argue. Kent finds a little empty basket and fills it with the most expensive confections in the display.

"You're just trying to buoy up my profit," I tell him.

"I'm just a glutton for gooey sweets," he says, patting his ample belly.

Mama and Kent exchange a glance that speaks of shared secrets and private jokes—an exchange so personal yet so guileless it's hard to mind being left out. I can't remember when I've seen Mama looking so happy. I'm glad for her. It's awfully nice to be glad instead of angry. *Awfully* nice. Surprising, too.

Before we know it we're into the dinner-hour rush. I don't even notice the sun dipping low or what have now become genuine hunger pangs in my stomach until suddenly a warm, rust-colored voice says over my shoulder, "Don't you think it's time you took a break for supper?" And there's Alex, looking every bit as put-together as he did this morning. He must have changed his clothes. He must have taken another shower. He smells like the same soap that has been wafting through my memory ever since we set up the booth this morning. I wonder how fast a heart has to beat before it stops being excitement and turns into a medical emergency.

"Go," Angela says, practically pushing me out of the booth. "Bonnie and I have eaten. Business is slowing down. We'll be fine."

Moments later, Alex and I are heading for the food table when the long hours and the heat and the lack of food catch up with me. My head gets a little swimmy and I sway a little. In the most natural way, as if he does this all the time, Alex takes me by the elbow and guides me down the hill. Normally I wouldn't lean on him the way I do, but he doesn't seem to mind.

The food smells wonderful. There's a choice of shredded pork barbecue on a bun or barbecued chicken on a plate. We both choose the chicken, which is fragrant and crisp from being basted on the grill with rich red barbecue sauce. There's also cole-slaw and baked beans and paper cups full of lemonade.

Because so many people are at the picnic tables near the cookers, we move off a little farther to a soft patch of grass on the other side of the bandstand. The music is subdued at this time of evening—it will rev up later—but now it's quiet enough to talk. Just as we veer off the path to sit down, Joey walks by, still with the two girls who'd come to get her earlier. She's so engrossed in lecturing to them that she doesn't notice us. "You have to grow it ten inches long before there's enough for a wig," we hear as they pass by. "If you have thick hair like I do, it can look just awful right before you get it cut. That's the sacrifice you make."

The two girls regard her worshipfully. "Do you think they'd take mine?" one of them asks. With great seriousness, Joey examines the girl's limp blond ponytail. By the time she speaks, a new band has begun to play and her words get lost in the sound.

Alex grins. "Do you think this means she's cured?" he asks as he sits down.

"Oh, yes. She'll probably go back to school and begin handing out a sign-up sheet. In a month or two, Locks of Love will be fending off hordes of twelve-year-old volunteers she's sent to them," I say. "She has the makings of a great activist."

"Or a crackerjack saleswoman," Alex says. "She had a very good teacher."

I lean back against the tree behind me, thinking yes. Yes, she did. The clear electronic music coming from the bandstand begins to unruffle my tattered nerves. I set my plate and cup of lemonade on a smooth spot in the grass. I'm hungry, but also half-asleep.

"Nice music," Alex says.

"Mmm." People wander by but don't seem to notice us. It's as if a gentle force-field has settled around us, letting us sit in privacy to shed the tension of the day. The air is soft and the music dances. I'm so relaxed that my next words come without my thinking. "I like the green pyramids rising."

I sit up with a start. I'm wide awake.

Alex pretends he doesn't notice. "Pyramids. Yes," he says mildly, like someone humoring a madwoman.

"I didn't mean—"

"Try the chicken," he says, intent on changing the subject. So far, both of our plates are untouched. He reaches for a drumstick and takes a bite.

From the face he makes, you would think he'd been poisoned.

"Alex?"

"I'm okay," he rasps, indicating that at least his airways are clear and he doesn't need CPR. When he speaks again, his voice is surprisingly normal. "The curlicues in this chicken need to be unwound."

"What?" It's a good thing we're sitting, because I would fall over otherwise. Never in my life have I known anyone but me who can taste the curlicues in chicken. It doesn't seem possible.

Then I know. It *isn't* possible. I've been betrayed.

"Joey told you," I say.

"Joey?"

"About my synesthesia."

"Joey knows?" He arches an eyebrow in surprise.

"Mama, then." I will not speak to Mama for the rest of my life.

"No. *No.*" Alex puts down his plate and takes my hand. I pull it away. "No one told me," he says. "I figured it out by myself. Remember that day your mother asked you to stay to dinner? After you were working in the garden? You mentioned the curlicues to her when you thought I wasn't listening."

"So?"

"So it reminded me of something, but I couldn't figure out what. Then I remembered a segment I'd seen on 60 *Minutes* about synesthesia. I did some research. There are whole books on the subject. I guess you know that. I kept waiting for you to say something about it and wondered why you never did. It's pretty interesting."

"Interesting the way an insect under glass is interesting."

"No." The way he says this, you'd think I'd insulted him.

"I never said anything," I explain, "because people generally think I'm crazy."

"I didn't think you were crazy." He frowns. "That would have been the last thing on my mind. I thought you were lucky to have that extra dimension of experience."

"Lucky!" Although in my secret heart of hearts, I do feel lucky, I would never say so. "If I'm so lucky, why are you making fun of me? Talking about curlicues in chicken as if you could taste them yourself!"

Alex's expression grows painfully earnest. "I didn't mean to make fun of you. I just didn't know how else to bring this up."

"Why bring it up at all? I mean, since I didn't bring it up myself."

Alex gives me a look of—well, longing.

"I thought it was important to get the subject out of the way. So we can go on from here."

"Go on from here?"

"As in…finishing this dinner we're having, for starters. And after you close your booth, listening to the rest of the band concert together. It can be our first date. Our second, if you count yesterday's lunch."

"Second," I say, because this sounds so much more substantial. Things can happen on a second date that might be problematic on a first. Obviously my closely held secret is not so closely held, considering all the people who now know about it. Why not test the waters?

When the time comes, Alex finds us a spot on the grass as far from the crowd as we can get and still hear. It's by far the best concert ever, though neither of us is exactly listening. Through band after band, we chatter as easily as we did all those nights on the phone, except face-to-face now, hands entwined, my thoughts so blurred by the nearness of his body you'd think I was sixteen. Now and then our shoulders touch; now and then our legs. My blood is as carbonated as it was yesterday at the restaurant, and I'm so dizzy you'd think we were drinking wine and not lemonade.

"Real lemons and lots of sugar," I tell Alex, explaining that this particular lemonade is as much a tradition at the barbecue as the chicken. "It probably has a million calories a cup." Then, forgetting myself, I say, "It tastes exactly like cool columns of glass."

Alex laughs, delighted rather than derisive. "How can that be?" he asks, his voice full of wonder. "Something tasting like cool columns of glass!" As if this is a subject that merits serious pondering.

"I can't explain it. It's like seeing the world in color when everyone else sees only black and white."

These are the words I used years ago to defend myself to Jeremy Taylor, who didn't get it. But Alex nods. "Yes," he says. "Yes."

For once, it's all right, really *all right*.

The band is playing beach music, ideal summer music, making me sway, sending translucent blue globes into the air. Alex takes my hand and pulls me up—to dance, I think. But I'm so wrong. He pulls me close against his chest, his face bending toward mine, enclosing us in a perfect circle.

His kiss is soft at first, then more urgent. A sharp, sweet jab of desire, and the blue globes of beach music giving way to pink-and-purple lightness I have not felt for twenty years. I hold on, wanting...so much, so quickly. But wait. Back then, there was no place for this to go. Now there is. We hold tight, our two bodies already melting into a future as solid as it is effervescent, more a promise than a color. There will be time for this—this summer and all the seasons to come. Ribbons of light dance in front of me, and it's as if I touch every one of them, just as they wrap us in a sunburst of raspberry sherbet.

||||| NASCAR

In February...

Collect all 4 debut novels in
the Harlequin NASCAR series.

SPEED DATING
by *USA TODAY* bestselling author
Nancy Warren

THUNDERSTRUCK
by Roxanne St. Claire

HEARTS UNDER CAUTION
by Gina Wilkins

DANGER ZONE
by Debra Webb

On sale
February
2007

And in May don't miss...

Gabby, a gutsy female NASCAR driver,
can't believe her mother is harping at her
again. How many times does she have
to say it? She's not going to help run the
family's corporation. She's not shopping
for a husband of the right pedigree. And
there's no way she's giving up racing!

SPEED BUMPS *is one of four
exciting Harlequin NASCAR books that
will go on sale in May.*

SEE COUPON INSIDE.

www.GetYourHeartRacing.com   NASCARMAY

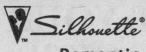

REQUEST YOUR FREE BOOKS!

**2 FREE NOVELS
PLUS 2
FREE GIFTS!**

There's the life you planned. And there's what comes next.

YES! Please send me 2 FREE Harlequin® NEXT™ novels and my 2 FREE mystery gifts. After receiving them, if I don't wish to receive any more books, I can return the shipping statement marked "cancel." If I don't cancel, I will receive 4 brand-new novels every other month and be billed just $3.99 per book in the U.S. or $4.74 per book in Canada, plus 25¢ shipping and handling per book plus applicable taxes, if any.* That's a savings of over 25% off the cover price! I understand that accepting the 2 free books and gifts places me under no obligation to buy anything. I can always return a shipment and cancel at any time. Even if I never buy anything from Harlequin, the two free books and gifts are mine to keep forever.   155 HDN EL33 355 HDN EL4F

Name	(PLEASE PRINT)	

Address		Apt. #

City	State/Prov.	Zip/Postal Code

Signature (if under 18, a parent or guardian must sign)

Order online at www.TryNEXTNovels.com

Or mail to the **Harlequin Reader Service®**:

IN U.S.A.: P.O. Box 1867, Buffalo, NY 14240-1867
IN CANADA: P.O. Box 609, Fort Erie, Ontario L2A 5X3

Not valid to current Harlequin NEXT subscribers.

Want to try two free books from another line?
Call 1-800-873-8635 or visit www.morefreebooks.com

* Terms and prices subject to change without notice. NY residents add applicable sales tax. Canadian residents will be charged applicable provincial taxes and GST. This offer is limited to one order per household. All orders subject to approval. Credit or debit balances in a customer's account(s) may be offset by any other outstanding balance owed by or to the customer. Please allow 4 to 6 weeks for delivery.

Your Privacy: Harlequin Books is committed to protecting your privacy. Our Privacy Policy is available online at www.eHarlequin.com or upon request from the Harlequin Reader Service. From time to time we make our lists of customers available to reputable firms who may have a product or service of interest to you. If you would prefer we not share your name and address, please check here. ☐

NEXT07R

LIKE MOTHER, LIKE DAUGHTER
(But In a Good Way)

with stories by
Jennifer Greene,
Nancy Robards Thompson
and Peggy Webb

Don't miss these three unforgettable stories
about the unbreakable—and sometimes
infuriating—bonds between mothers and
daughters and the men who get caught in
the madness (when they're not causing it!).

HARLEQUIN®

COMING NEXT MONTH

#83 LAST NIGHT AT THE HALFMOON •
Kate Austin
When Aimee King learns that the Halfmoon Drive-In is
closing, it feels like the end of the world to her. Sure she
loves her life: her son, her job, her parents who live down
the street, even her ex-husband. But with the closing, she's
about to learn there's something more important uniting all
the people in her life....

**#84 LIKE MOTHER, LIKE DAUGHTER
(BUT IN A GOOD WAY)** • Jennifer Greene,
Nancy Robards Thompson and Peggy Webb
Don't miss these three unforgettable stories about the
unbreakable—and sometimes infuriating—bonds between
mothers and daughters and the men who get caught in the
madness (when they're not causing it!).

NXTCNM0407